Dear mouse friends,
Welcome to the world of

Geronimo Stilton

THE RODENT'S GAZETTE
EDITORIAL STAFF

Geronimo Stilton
A learned and brainy
mouse; editor of
The Rodent's Gazette

Thea Stilton
Geronimo's sister and
special correspondent at
The Rodent's Gazette

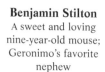

Trap Stilton
An awful joker;
Geronimo's cousin and
owner of the store
Cheap Junk for Less

Benjamin Stilton
A sweet and loving
nine-year-old mouse;
Geronimo's favorite
nephew

Geronimo Stilton

A FABUMOUSE SCHOOL ADVENTURE

Scholastic Inc.

New York   Toronto   London   Auckland
Sydney   Mexico City   New Delhi   Hong Kong

ISBN-13: 978-0-545-02138-8

ISBN-10: 0-545-02138-3

Stilton is the name of a famous English cheese. It is a registered trademark of the Stilton Cheese Makers' Association. For more information, go to www.stiltoncheese.com.

Text by Geronimo Stilton
Original title *A Scuola di Formaggio*
Cover by Giuseppe Ferrario
Illustrations by Alessandro Pastrovicchio
Graphics by Merenguita Gingermouse and Yuko Egusa

Special thanks to Kristin Earhart
Special thanks to Lidia Morson Tramontozzi
Interior design by Kay Petronio

12 11 10 9 8 7 6 5 4   10 11 12 13 14/0

Printed in the U.S.A.   40
First printing, July 2009

A VERY SPECIAL MORNING

It's true. I am not a morning mouse. But one FALL day, things got off to an especially bad start. Maybe it was because my **alarm clock** went off too early, or because I had to skip breakfast. Then again, maybe it was

because I was in a mad rush. That morning just started off on the wrong paw: It was a typical **BAD DAY**. You know what I mean. It was one of those days when anything that could go wrong, did go wrong.

I'm the kind of mouse who likes a routine. In the morning, I wake up slowly, stretch lazily, cuddle back under my covers, and lounge for a while. I like to pick out my clothes carefully and then eat a **hearty**, leisurely breakfast before I leave for work.

I'm not the kind of mouse who JUMPS

CEREAL

TOAST WITH JAM

MILK

FRUIT

out of bed at the crack of dawn and immediately **starts** doing yoga. No way!

As I was saying, that morning things seemed to be extra topsy-turvy.

First, the alarm clock went off extra early. It rang at 6:30 A.M., an hour before I usually get up! I stretched my arm, turned it off, and turned over to catch a few more ZZZs. I couldn't even think about getting up. It was

I'm **NOT** like this!

I'm like this!

just too early. But I knew I had to force myself out of bed, because it was a very **special** day for my nephew Benjamin! It was **CaReeR DaY** at his school, and I had been invited to be a guest speaker. On Career Day, different people come in to talk about their jobs, and I was going to tell Benjamin's class about mine.

Oops, I'm sorry. I haven't told you what I do. I'm a **writer**, editor, and publisher. I publish the most famouse newspaper on Mouse Island, *The Rodent's Gazette.* Everybody in New Mouse City reads it! My name is Stilton, *Geronimo Stilton.*

If you want to know the truth, the thought of speaking in front of Benjamin's friends, his teachers, and the other guests made my tail quiver. It made my whiskers shaky and

4

my paws soggy with **sweat**! I'm a very shy mouse and I get terrible stage fright when I have to speak in front of people. I stammer and mix up words. I become clumsy. I get so frazzled I usually make a FOOL of myself! Nevertheless, I knew it was a very special day for Benjamin. I'd jump through flaming hoops for my nephew! I had to be super cool and smart, too.

"I'll make Benjamin proud!"

I'M NOT A MORNING MOUSE!

I was already stressed out about my speech. To ease my nerves, I took a deep breath and **repeated** these words: *I will not embarrass Benjamin. I am a smart, successful mouse.*

I was starting to relax when the phone rang. I jumped up to answer it and bumped my head on the shelf over my bed. **Ouch!** What a nasty wake-up call!

Ouch!

I answered the phone. It was my sister, **Thea**.

"Geronimo, you're still in bed, aren't you?" she said. "**Hurry up!** Don't you remember what day it is? Please, try not to look like a fool in front of everybody. "**Benjamin looks up to you!**"

"I'm awake (almost)," I muttered. "And, of course, I remember what day it is! Don't worry, I have no intention of looking like a fool (but I usually end up looking like one anyway)."

I hung up the phone and sighed. Now I was nervous all over again! I repeated my mousetra* aloud: "I will not embarrass Benjamin. I am a smart, successful mouse."

When I finally found the oomph to get up,

---

* A *mousetra*, like a *mantra*, is a phrase that you repeat to give yourself comfort or confidence.

it was 6:50. I had to move like a mouse in a rat race! That's when my cell phone rang. It was **Grandfather William**.

"Geronimo! Are you ready?" he asked. "You're not going to be late, are you? Of all days, not today! And I beg you, please don't make a fool of yourself. *"Benjamin really looks up to you.*

"And above all, remember: The family's *good name* is at stake here, as well as that of *The Rodent's Gazette*!"

My whiskers got all in a knot just listening to him.

"OF COURSE, Grandfather," I answered. "I know Benjamin looks up to me."

I tried to cut him off, but he went on and on for a full **TEN MINUTES**! I had just hung up when the doorbell rang.

It was Aunt Sweetfur.

"Good morning, Geronimo," she said. "I was just passing by and thought I'd stop in to say hello. I hope it's not a bad time."

"Thank you, Aunt Sweetfur," I replied. "No, you're not bothering me at all. Come right in."

"I brought you something sweet to give you a little **courage**. I know how hard it is for you to talk in front of a crowd. But, please, try to do your very best. **Benjamin looks up to you!"**

"It's always a pleasure talking with you, Aunt Sweetfur, and your **sweets** are such a treat," I told her.

She stopped in for ten minutes, which was enough time to leave me cheesecake cookies, a warm smile, and a couple of tips.

I was looking forward to *savoring* a rich and creamy cookie when I got a **text message**.

It was from *Petunia Pretty Paws*.

Petunia's cell phone

Hi, G. Break a leg today. Benjamin looks up to you. See you soon.

Wow, Petunia was so sweet to text me. And she had written *"See you soon!"*

Hmm, could it mean maybe, just maybe, she wanted to see me?

With my head swirling in the clouds, I began daydreaming about her. I started to **text** Petunia back, but my paws were all clammy. Just thinking about her made my fingers feel like jelly. When I looked down to see what I had typed, it was all a jumble:

Geronimo's cell phone

> Thiks, i hop toes eeyew son zoo.

I had wanted to write: "Thanks, I hope to see you soon, too," but I was so jittery, my fingers kept SLIPPING on the keys. I went to erase the message, but I accidentally punched the SEND button! **What bad luck.** Why me?

Then the doorbell rang again. This time it was **Trap**! He whipped into the house like a Tasmanian devil!

"Gerry, Gerry, quite contrary, why aren't

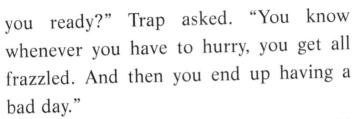

you ready?" Trap asked. "You know whenever you have to hurry, you get all frazzled. And then you end up having a bad day."

"If you would leave me alone so I could get ready, I wouldn't have to rush," I said.

"Are you **nervous**?" he asked.

"No, I'm **NOT** nervous."

"See. You are **nervous**. It's a bad case of jitters, I tell you."

"I said **NO**, I'm not nervous."

"Are you sure?" Trap prodded. "Because when you get nervous, you **ALWAYS** make a fool of yourself."

"I'm **NOT** nervous! But if you don't let me get ready, I'm going to —"

"Calm down," Trap said. "I told you, you're **nervous**. Just try to relax, or we're all going to end up looking silly."

"Enooough, I get it!" I screeched.

When I finally got rid of Trap, it was **7:50**. Now I really *was* late! Benjamin said he'd wait for me at his school bus stop at 8:00.

Yikes! I wasn't ready and I had run out of time!

I quickly washed my face, dressed, and ran outside . . . without eating my breakfast!

It was definitively turning out to be a **BAD DAY**!

DEFINITELY A BAD DAY

I'm so sleepy!

The alarm clock went off too early: at 6:30 A.M.!

When the phone rang, I was startled and hit my head on the bookshelf.

Ouch!

I beg you!

I get it!

Aunt Sweetfur brought me some whisker-licking sweets that I didn't have time to eat!

Luckily, I got a text message from my friend Petunia Pretty Paws!

Trap stormed in and made me even more nervous than before!

THANKS, I PREFER GETTING CARSICK

I got to the bus stop just in the nick of time. As soon as Benjamin saw me, he gave me a **HIGH FIVE** that made my paw sting! He was so excited that I almost forgot that I was having a **BAD DAY**. I even forgot that I hadn't eaten breakfast!

He grabbed my jacket, dragged me to the **back** of the bus, and sat me down in his favorite seat in the very last row. When I was a little *mouseling*, I could never sit in the back of the bus: I threw up every time I tried!

But I didn't say anything to Benjamin: I wanted the day to be very **special** for him. I couldn't let him down! So I sat in the back of the bus and crossed my whiskers

that I wouldn't get sick. Unfortunately, my stomach was as empty as a cookie jar after a mouseling birthday party, and I always get queasy when I'm hungry.

In fact, as soon as the bus **TOOK OFF** bumping and thumping, my stomach started sloshing.

After the first curve, I was as **WHITE** as a ghost.

After the second curve, I was as **GREEN** as pistachio ice cream.

After the third curve, I felt dismally dizzy.

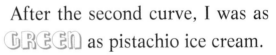

WHAT A GHASTLY RIDE!

Then the bus hit a pothole, and a loose *spring* in the seat poked me right in the tail. I yelped and **jumped up**, landing two rows up, right in between a cute pigtailed mouseling and a freckle-faced mouseling. I

was wedged between them like slice of Swiss on a grilled cheese sandwich. Their squeaky voices poked holes right through my eardrums.

WHAT A GHASTLY RIDE!

"Are you Stilton, *Geronimo Stilton*?" the freckle-faced mouseling asked.

"Is it really you?" asked the pigtailed mouseling.

Are you Stilton?

Is it really you?

"Is it really, really you? Are you the one who writes all those books?"

I smiled, pleased with myself.

"Of course it's me!" I insisted.

"Good," the boy mouseling said. "I wanted to tell you that on page twenty-seven of your last B O O K, there is a **mistake** in the seventh word on the fifteenth line. You spelled 'cheese' with only one **e**! I'm surprised — I never expected it from you!"

The girl mouseling had to have her say as well. "It's true! I saw it, too! My aunt is best friends with Sally Ratmousen's hairdresser's sister, and she said that Sally said that it was just **scandalous**!"

Hmph. Sally Ratmousen was the publisher of *The Daily Rat,* my paper's competitor. Leave it to her to be catty. I tried to change the subject, but the little mouselings would not stop. I can't stand gossip!

WHAT A GHASTLY TRIP!

Luckily, Benjamin came to my rescue.

"Come on, Uncle Geronimo," he said. "I want to introduce you to my friends."

I was about to follow him to our seat in the back of the bus when the two mouselings stopped me.

"Stay here, Mr. Stilton," they said. "If you sit in the back, you might throw up. You know who told me that you get CARSICK? My neighbor's sister's . . ."

I felt my stomach grumble and growl. I wondered if I should stay with the two gossipy, catty, extra-chatty mouselings.

I decided I would rather get carsick!

GERONIMO STILTON . . .
"PRESENT!"

I took a seat at the back of the bus, hoping I wouldn't feel queasy again.

"Hang on, Uncle Geronimo," Benjamin reassured me. "We're almost there!"

The trip seemed **ENDLESS**.

A curve to the left . . . A curve to the right . . . .

A CURVE TO THE LEFT

A CURVE TO THE RIGHT

BANG!
BANG! BANG!

The school bus did another **three curves to the right and four curves to the left**. A couple of beastly bumps made me hit my head on the roof! In the meantime, Benjamin was busy showing me the **SCHEDULE** for the morning at Little Tails Academy. I couldn't bear to look at it: I was woefully woozy! (I always get sick when I read in a moving vehicle.)

Here, read it yourselves:

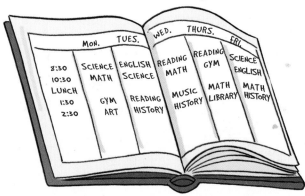

	MON.	TUES.	WED.	THURS.	FRI.
8:30	SCIENCE	ENGLISH	READING	READING	SCIENCE
10:30	MATH	SCIENCE	MATH	GYM	ENGLISH
LUNCH					
1:30	GYM	READING	MUSIC	MATH	MATH
2:30	ART	HISTORY	HISTORY	LIBRARY	HISTORY

When I finally got off the bus, my head was spinning as if I had just gotten off the tallest, most rickety roller coaster of all time.

THERE WAS NO DOUBT, IT WAS A BAD DAY.

I stumbled toward the school. As soon as I stepped through the doors, a thousand memories came flooding back.

They were such **happy** memories! I learned **SO MUCH**! I got into so much mischief! I made so many *friends*: Hercule Poirat, my detective friend; Kornelius von Kickpaw (*he's Secret Agent 00K, but don't tell anyone!*); and, obviously, my **joke-loving** cousin Trap.

And then there was Veronica Stiffwhiskers, my sworn enemy at Little Tails Academy. She was such a **cute** rodent, perfect in every way, and good at everything. Too good. The

school had never seen such rivals as the two of us. We competed in everything, and she always won.

I stopped in front of the school's display case. I looked at all the students' plaques, **medals**, and **trophies**. Her name was everywhere! Veronica Stiffwhiskers, Veronica Stiffwhiskers, Veronica Stiffwhiskers.

She **WON** the math challenge, the spelling bee, and the essay contest, and I always got *second prize*. Second prize wasn't that bad, but I would have loved to be numero uno just once!

For years, I dreamed of having my name

on a plaque or trophy in that display case. I sighed and walked away, feeling a little sad. I tried to console myself that, in spite of being number two, I had done quite well for myself: I'm the editor in chief and publisher of a newspaper, I have lots of friends, and I even won the Ratitzer Prize. Despite all of that, though, I still would have liked to see my ⟨ NAME ⟩ inside that case.

While these thoughts were rumbling through my head, Benjamin led me through the halls to his classroom.

The school had changed so much!

It was the same, but very different.

It was more **MODERN**: It had a computer lab, a new gymnasium, language and music labs, an auditorium, and a spectacular art room. Everything was state-of-the-art!

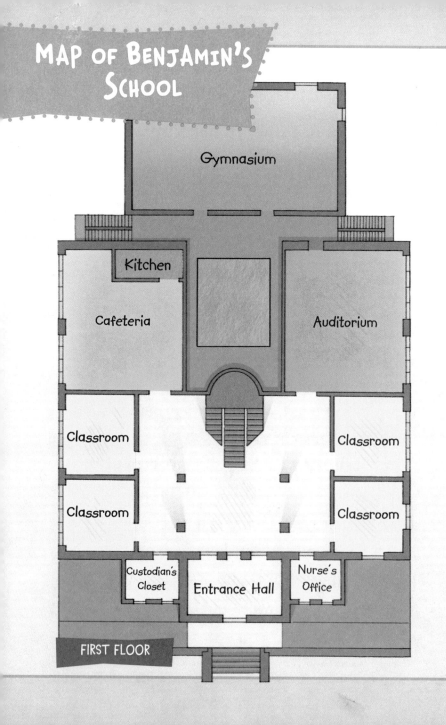

MAP OF BENJAMIN'S SCHOOL

Gymnasium

Kitchen

Cafeteria

Auditorium

Classroom

Classroom

Classroom

Classroom

Custodian's Closet

Entrance Hall

Nurse's Office

FIRST FLOOR

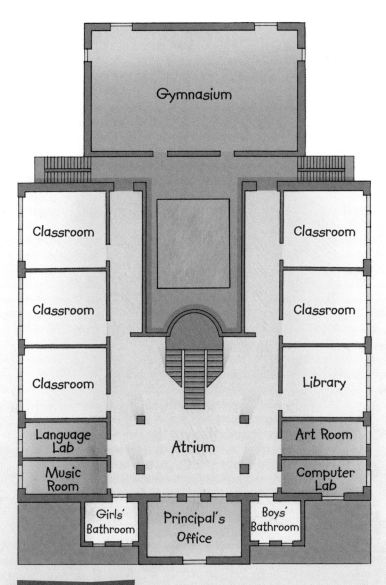

Gymnasium

Classroom

Classroom

Classroom

Language Lab

Music Room

Classroom

Classroom

Library

Art Room

Computer Lab

Atrium

Girls' Bathroom

Principal's Office

Boys' Bathroom

SECOND FLOOR

LIKE MICE IN A CHEESE FACTORY!

Looking at all those rooms, I longed for the days when I scampered along those halls with my friends. We had such adventures, like little mice in a big cheese factory!

But I didn't have any time to revel in my memories. Benjamin was pushing me into his classroom.

"Here we are, Uncle Geronimo!"

A rodent with long blonde hair and blue eyes came toward me. It was Miss Angel Paws, Benjamin's teacher.

She greeted me with a bright smile.

"Mr. Stilton, it's such a pleasure to have you with us today!" she exclaimed.

"Good morning, Miss Angel Paws," I

replied as I reached out to shake her paw.
"Thank you for inviting me. It's a pleasure
to see you again. **And good morning
to you, class!**"

I looked around and recognized the smiling
faces of Benjamin's friends.

I knew them all because we had taken a
ratastic field trip to **Niagara Falls** together.

It felt good to be with the class, and I
was starting to think that maybe my luck

Miss Angel Paws!

had changed when a voice came over the loudspeaker.

 ringgg!

"Miss Angel Paws, please come to the principal's office immediately."

The voice sounded very familiar, but I couldn't figure out *why*. Miss Angel Paws smiled at me.

"Geronimo, I'm leaving you **in charge**," she said. "Would you please take attendance? If I don't come back within a few minutes, please take the students to the playground. Today our class is scheduled **TO RAISE THE SCHOOL FLAG**: It's a real honor. Oh, and **Spike**, our class pet, needs to be fed. That's about it. Is everything clear?"

I never say no to someone in need, so I nodded confidently.

"Don't worry," I said gallantly. "I'll take care of everything!"

As soon as the words came out of my mouth, I regretted it. I didn't have a clue how to lead a class. I had never taken attendance. I didn't know how to raise the flag. I couldn't remember who was **who**. And, I was afraid to ask: **What was** Spike?

It was too late. She was gone, and I was left to deal with things.

LIKE A FLAG
IN THE WIND

I decided to start with the attendance.

I found the list of names and began to read them in alphabetical order: "Antonia."

"Here!"

"Benjamin."

"Uncle Geronimo, you know I'm here," he giggled. "You brought me to school! Of course I'm here!"

Everybody laughed and I turned as red as my tie. I quickly cleared my throat and tried to move on.

"Ahem, good. I wanted to make sure you were paying attention."

I went ahead with the rest of the attendance. Everything went well until late in the alphabet.

"Malcolm."

"Here!"

"Mohamed."

"Here!"

"Oliver."

"Here!"

"Punk Rat."

"ABSENT."

"What do you mean, absent?" I asked. "I recognize you from our field trip. You're Punk Rat! I remember you."

What do you mean, absent?

In fact, I remembered him a little too well. How could I have forgotten him?

During our trip to Niagara Falls, he got into all kinds of trouble. And he blamed me!

"No, I'm not Punk Rat," he replied. "I'm his twin brother!"

"Don't try to fool me, Punk Rat."

"I told you. I'm not Punk Rat. I'm his twin, MODEST MOUSE. We decided to switch schools for the day."

Everybody laughed, and I became bright red all over again. Nevertheless, I decided to play along with his game.

"Okay, Modest Mouse, I'll write your name in the attendance book. Punk Rat is absent. Modest Mouse is present. So, Modest Mouse, since you are our newest student, you will

have the honor of raising the flag. Do you think you can do that?" I asked.

"Of course I can," he replied. "I can do anything. I'm the type of mouse who likes to help out. Raising a flag is easy. Every mouse scout knows how to do it, unless he or she is so **old** that he or she has forgotten."

Everybody *laughed*, and I became **redder** than ever because it was true. I couldn't remember how to raise a flag! And even though Modest Mouse seemed to  be acting nice, I had a feeling Punk Rat had a trick up his tail.

"Why, oh why, doesn't the teacher come back?" I muttered to myself as I tried to get the class under control again.

I finished roll call without another mishap

and then I took the class outside. We made a circle around the flagpole and got ready to raise the flag. I became very confused as I watched Punk Rat fumble with the hooks and pulley. I couldn't figure it out. The next thing I knew, Punk Rat pulled on the cord. As the flag went up the pole, I went right along with it!

I was waving like a flag in the wind!

"**Help!** Can somebody get me down from here?" I shouted. "I'm afraid of heights!"

The custodian came running out. He looked very worried. "Hang in there, Mr. Stilton!"

He immediately pulled me down.

"Are you okay, Mr. Stilton?" he asked. "It's such an honor to meet you. I'm glad you flagged me down."

Hearing that word, I blushed again.

"Um, sorry," he said.

??? WHERE'S SPIKE?

I looked at the custodian's *calm* face, brown eyes, and **kind**, wide smile.

His face seemed very familiar to me, as if I had known him all my life.

"Do we **know** each other?" I asked.

He smiled. "No, you don't know me, but I know all about you," he replied. "I'm **HENRY HANDIPAWS**, the custodian here."

"Well, thank you for all your help," I said. "You really saved me, Mr. Handipaws."

I turned to face Punk Rat. **"Punk Rat, we need to have a chat,"** I said sternly.

He looked at me **INNOCENTLY** with his wide brown eyes.

"I'm not Punk Rat," he claimed. "Punk Rat is absent. I'm Modest Mouse, his twin. I'm a good mouse. I didn't do it on purpose!"

I didn't have proof, but I was certain the little rodent had his **paws** on the flag fiasco.

Anyway, I knew we should get back to the classroom. We still needed to feed Spike, and I wanted to make a good impression on Benjamin's teacher. As soon as we entered the room, Antonia

came forward. She had a proud smile on her snout.

"Today is my turn to **feed** Spike," she said.

"Good. Why don't you take care of it right away?" I suggested. "By the way, what kind of animal is Spike?"

There was no need for anyone to tell me. Unfortunately, I found out all by myself!

As soon as Antonia opened the cage, something leaped out at *LIGHTNING* speed.

Everyone screeched as Spike, **terrified** by the students' screams, sped across the classroom floor. Spike zigzagged under the desks, circled the cubby holes, and then ran straight up my pant leg, climbed under my vest, and popped out of my collar!

I gasped in surprise. Spike was a scaly green **GECKO**!

ALL ABOUT GECKOS

WHAT IS A GECKO?
The gecko, a member of the reptile family, is a lizard. It is small and scaly. Its body is covered with scales that can change color to mimic the surrounding environment. Although most geckos are nocturnal, some species are active during the day.

HOW BIG IS A GECKO?
A gecko's body can measure from 3/4 inch to 16 inches long, depending on the species.

WHAT DOES A GECKO EAT?
Geckos eat insects.

WHERE DO GECKOS LIVE?
Geckos live in all warm and temperate zones on the earth. They are especially prominent in regions of Central and South America, Africa, Australia, and the Mediterranean, and in the southern part of Asia.

INTERESTING FACT: To catch prey, geckos can stay motionless for several minutes. When the prey comes close, the gecko will suddenly attack with a quick snap.

INTERESTING SKILLS: Geckos can climb wherever they want. Their toes have fleshy pads on the tips that will stick to anything — even smooth walls. At night, they like to stay close to a light so that they can feed on insects that are attracted to it.

DO YOU KNOW? The gecko is considered a domesticated animal because it can be raised in a terrarium. The terrarium needs to have light to provide warmth. It also should have a hiding place, so that the gecko feels safe. Don't forget a small bowl of water and some insects for the gecko to eat.

???
CAN ANYTHING ELSE GO WRONG?

Spike was **tickling** me, and I couldn't stop squirming around. The gecko jumped off my elbow, zoomed across the room, and jumped out a window. The students all **SCREAMED**! That's when the classroom door opened.

Miss Angel Paws walked in, followed by four other rodents. They looked as though

they were also there for Career Day. As soon as the teacher came into the room, the entire class QUIETED down. She gave me a long look, and **I turned purple with embarrassment**.

Antonia's eyes swelled up with tears. "Spike ran away," she sobbed. "He's gone forever!"

"Don't worry, we'll find him later," said Miss Angel Paws. "Now I want to **introduce** you to our other guests: Professor Sandsnout, renowned Egyptologist; Miss Lulu Soufflé, inventor of SMALL-HOLED Swiss cheese; Professor Miles Magmamouse, volcanologist; and the world-famous actor Robert Rodentford."

On hearing that name, the class clapped enthusiastically.

CAREER DAY

NAME: Cyril T.

LAST NAME: Sandsnout

NICKNAME: The Desert Rat

PROFESSION: Egyptologist

HIS HOBBY: He has an incredible collection of joke books. He loves to tell jokes and to play pranks, too!

NAME: Miles

LAST NAME: Magmamouse

NICKNAME: Lava Lover

PROFESSION: Volcanologist

HIS HOBBY: Ever since he was a little mouseling, he has always loved doing experiments. However, he has almost set his lab on fire on more than one occasion.

NAME: Lulu

LAST NAME: Soufflé

NICKNAME: Gouda

PROFESSION: Chef

HER HOBBY: Making cheese! She has invented many mouthwatering new cheeses, including her famouse small-holed Swiss.

NAME: Robert

LAST NAME: Rodentford

NICKNAME: Blondie

PROFESSION: Actor

HIS HOBBY: He loves nature and animals, and has ten dogs! Horses run wild on his ranch.

Help! A Mummy!

Miss Angel Paws asked **Professor Sandsnout**, one of my dear old friends, to speak to the class. He immediately started talking about his work.

"Students, I'm an Egyp-tol-o-gist. That means I'm an expert on ancient Egypt. I'm also the director of the Egyptian Mouseum in New Mouse City. Have any of you ever visited the mouseum?"

There was a chorus of mouselings all shouting, "I DID! I DID!"

Just thinking about that mouseum made me shiver. I'm terrified of sarcophaguses and I'm especially scared of **MUMMIES**! (Don't tell anyone, but that mouseum gives me nightmares!)

Professor Sandsnout proudly placed a **MYst𝖊rl0us**, old wooden sarcophagus on the desk. It was shaped like a cat.

"OOOOOOOOOOOOOOH!" said the class.

The lid looked heavy. Professor Sandsnout lifted it with both hands. **CREEEEEAK!**

"AAAAAAAAAAAAAAH!" whispered the class.

Suddenly, the lid slipped from Professor Sandsnout's fingers. **BANG!**

"Yeee-oooow!" I screeched.

Yeee-oooow!

The lid had FALLEN on my paw!

THIS DAY WAS BEYOND BAD!

When the professor began to pick up the **sarcophagus** lid, I quickly moved away, just in case.

That's when I saw Spike.

I tried to grab him, but he skidded through my legs, ran around the room, and climbed straight up the wall!!

Knowing I couldn't catch Spike, I turned back to Professor Sandsnout. He had put something new on the desk— a cat mummy! **"Aaaack!"** I screeched. There's only one thing that scares me more than mummies, and it's **CATS**!

I felt dizzy. I backed away. I tried to find something to grab on to. I didn't want to faint in front of the class! I felt a hand, and I reached for it. But it wasn't someone's hand, it was a bone. In fact, it was a pile of **BONES**!

MUMMIES

The ancient Egyptians believed in life after death. When a person died, they preserved the body and its internal organs for the trip to the afterlife. To preserve the body, they used a technique called MUMMIFICATION.

How were mummies made?

Mummification was a very long and detailed process that took seventy days. First, all the internal organs except the heart were removed and placed inside special containers, called canopic jars. The heart was left inside the body. Then, to dry the body, the skin was covered with a special salt called natron.

Next, the sunken body was filled with linen, oil, and aromatic herbs to make it appear lifelike. Finally, it was wrapped in linen. Sometimes, a funeral mask was placed on the face of the mummy.

INTERESTING FACTS

The ancient Egyptians worshipped many gods and goddesses. One was Bastet, the cat goddess. Egyptians believed cats were sacred. When cats died, they were also mummified.

"Aaaack!" I screeched again.

I was so terrified, I almost ran out the door. Suddenly, my friend Professor Sandsnout grabbed me by the collar.

"Geronimo, where are you going?" he asked. "This guys's been dead for thousands of years! He's not going to hurt you!"

Well, I never said I wasn't a 'FRAIDY MOUSE.

AN EXPLOSIVE EXPERIMENT

Luckily, Professor Sandsnout put the cat mummy and all those **BONES** back into the sarcophagus. His talk was over. I sighed with relief. Now I could listen to the next guest, PROFESSOR MILES MAGMAMOUSE.

Professor Magmamouse lowered the shades and put on a video that explained everything any mouse would ever want to know about volcanoes, volcanic eruptions, and earthquakes.

WHAT AN EXCITING LINE OF WORK!

He had seen hundreds of volcanoes and lots of lava in his life.

Suddenly, my job seemed wimpy and BORING.

MAKE A VOLCANIC ERUPTION WITH MILES MAGMAMOUSE!

WHAT YOU'LL NEED:
- 16-ounce plastic bottle
- Cardboard base, approximately 3 feet by 3 feet
- Glue
- Brown modeling clay (enough to sculpt a mountain)
- Warm water
- Baking soda
- Liquid dish soap
- Red food coloring (optional)
- A funnel
- Vinegar

WHAT YOU'LL DO: Be sure to ask an adult for help before you begin. To limit the mess, make your volcano outside or on a large table with a protective covering.

1. Glue the plastic bottle to the center of the cardboard base.

2. Mold the brown modeling clay around the bottle to form a volcano.

3. Mix ½ cup water, ¼ cup baking soda, and one spoonful of liquid dish soap together. Use the funnel to help you pour the mixture into the bottle, which will become the mouth of your volcano. Add three drops of food coloring if desired.

4. Add three drops of vinegar to the mouth of the volcano, and enjoy the eruption!

When the baking soda mixes with the vinegar, it forms a foam that looks just like the lava in a volcanic eruption.

At some point, Professor Magmamouse asked me to give him a hand with the **EXPERIMENT**. I listened closely because I didn't want to mess up. I had to look good for Benjamin!

"Geronimo, when I say NOW, put three drops of vinegar into the mouth of the volcano," Professor Magmamouse told me. "It is important you only add three drops. Is that clear?"

At that moment, my nose began to itch. I tried to hold my breath, but I couldn't stop myself from sneezing.

"**AAAAchoooo!**"

And that's how I poured the entire bottle of vinegar into the volcano. It erupted, and lava oozed everywhere!

What a mess!

Luckily, Henry Handipaws, the custodian, arrived at once. He had a huge pail of cleaning supplies. He gave me one look and pulled out his biggest bRoOm.

"Some people would blow their top over a mess like this," Henry commented. "But don't worry, Mr. Stilton, I'll get you **squeaky clean** in no time! You want to look extra spiffy today." Then he winked at me.

Help!

There. All done!

CHEESE TASTING!

Mr. Handipaws finished cleaning me off just in time for me to hear **Lulu Soufflé**'s presentation.

She was such a *fascinating* rodent! Her skin was as pale as mozzarella. Her hair was long and silky.

I could not take my **EYES** — or **ears** — off of her.

Lulu was telling the class that she hadn't been a great student.

"When I was a little *mouseling*, my favorite subject in school was lunch," she said. "Nothing made me *happier* than munching on a piece of **perfectly aged cheese**. That's why I decided to make food my profession."

63

She knew **everything** about cheese. Lulu was sharper than New Mouse–style cheddar!

I could have listened to her all day. After all, cheese is one of my **favorite** subjects, especially when I'm hungry!

The best part of the presentation was when Lulu declared that she had talked enough. "Tasting is **believing**, so let's have a snack," she announced.

She lifted up a platter of all kinds of cheeses. **Yum, yum!** I picked an enormous piece of cheese that had a funny smell and a greenish blue color. I was about to wolf it down when Lulu spoke.

"See, Mr. Stilton is about to taste a piece of blue cheese that is made from a special kind of mold—"

LULU'S EASY CHEESY PIZZA FONDUE

WHAT YOU'LL NEED:

- 1 (26 ounce) jar pasta sauce (without meat)
- 2 cups shredded mozzarella cheese
- ¼ cup shredded Parmesan cheese
- 2 teaspoons dried oregano
- 1 teaspoon garlic pepper
- ½ teaspoon onion powder
- 1 loaf French or Italian bread, cut into cubes

WHAT YOU'LL DO:

1. In a two-quart pot or a slow cooker, combine the pasta sauce, cheeses, and spices.

2. Cook until cheese is melted and sauce is hot.

3. Be careful not to let it burn around the edges.

4. To eat, dip bread cubes in fondue and enjoy!

"Mold????" I asked, quickly pulling the cheese away from my snout.

She smiled. "Of course," she said. "To make blue cheese, you use milk, milk enzymes, and molds like these."

She placed a little **BOTTLE** of a greenish, bluish, vile-smelling substance right under my nose.

The aroma was so disgusting, that *I* turned greenish blue, then white, and then I fainted!

He's such a wimp!

When I came to, Lulu seemed very concerned.

"I'm surprised you have such a weak stomach, Mr. Stilton," she said. "I really thought you were a mouse of GREAT COURAGE. And to think that I wanted you to help me cook my triple-decker, super-duper cheese SANDWICH for everyone's lunch!"

I didn't want her to think I was a wimp. I jumped up.

"Not at all, Miss Lulu. Please, let me help you!"

But then I caught another whiff of the mold and I FAINTED again! HOW EMBARRASSING!

MISS LULU'S SPECIALTY

This time, I came to with some help from Punk Rat. He emptied an entire vase of **water** from the teacher's desk right on my head!

Brrr! The water was freezing!

At least I was able to walk with Lulu to the school kitchen to help her make some of her famouse triple-decker cheese sandwiches.

I really wanted to make a good impression because:

(1) I was hungry and I wanted to sample some nonmoldy cheese.

(2) Lulu was very charming and I never refuse to help a kind rodent, especially one who is so cute!

(3) Did I mention I was hungry? I had to eat

something, or else I would faint . . . again!

Sadly, sneaking a treat was not so easy. I tried dipping my finger into the cheese sauce, but Lulu caught me.

"I thought you had better *manners*, Mr. Stilton!" she scolded. "You should never sample a recipe until the cook says it's ready. It's RUDE!"

I became **PINK** with embarrassment and didn't dare taste anything else, even as I made **757** triple-decker sandwiches.

Every sandwich had three layers. I spread each layer of bread with Lulu's delicious special cheese sauce.

 x **757 times = ...**

Go ahead, you tell me how many slices of bread I spread in total. I was never good in math.

Then I cut **757** slices of turkey, and topped each sandwich with a cherry tomato, an olive, and a little New Mouse City flag. And I did that 757 times! And did I say how many times I accidentally stuck my paws with toothpicks? **359**!

GERONIMO'S GRILLED CHEESE MASTERPIECE

I'M no chef, but I made my own version of Lulu's sandwich at home. Ask an adult to help you make this cheeserific treat. It's super tasty! Yum!

WHAT YOU'LL NEED:

- Butter
- two slices bread (not too thick!)
- three slices cheese (any combination of mozzarella, cheddar, American, gruyere, Havarti, Swiss, or provolone)
- smoked sliced turkey deli meat (one slice)
- pepperoni (four small slices)

WHAT YOU'LL DO:

① Spread butter on one side of each slice of bread.

② With an adult's help, place a skillet over medium-low heat. Put one slice of bread in the skillet, butter side down.

③ Place two pieces of cheese on top of the bread. Next add the turkey and pepperoni, and then the final piece of cheese. Place the second piece of bread, butter side up, on top.

④ When the cheese starts to melt and the bottom piece of bread turns golden brown, flip the sandwich with a spatula. When the second piece of bread is golden brown, it's done!

* Hint: If you have a sandwich press or a waffle maker, you can make this sandwich without a skillet.

As soon as we finished the sandwiches, we took them to the cafeteria for our ravenous mouselings. Of course, the food was a great *success*.

The sandwiches were so good that, when it was my turn to serve myself, there were only **crumbs** left on the tray. I was so frustrated, I wanted to scream! I was sooooo **HUNGRY**, I could have eaten the toothpicks!

Because Lulu was **LOOKING** at me, I acted like nothing was wrong. I had made a fool of myself enough already.

PLEASE, UNTANGLE MY PAWS!

After lunch (What lunch? I hadn't eaten anything. Sigh!), Benjamin and his friends had **RECESS** while the adults cleaned up the cafeteria.

I finished washing the dishes, and boy did I need a rest! That's when I heard that same familiar voice over the loudspeaker,

 *ringgg!*

"Miss Angel Paws, please report to the principal's office right away."

I was sure I recognized that voice. Where, oh WHERE, had I heard it before?

Miss Angel Paws asked me to **SUB** for her again.

"Geronimo, would you please keep an eye on the mouselings on the playground?"

I wanted to ask: "why me!?!? Why not Robert Rodentford, who's been sitting there sunning himself for the last hour while I made the lunch, served the meal, and scoured the tables???"

But Miss Angel Paws was already gone, and I had to:

1. Rescue **one** mouseling who was about to fall from a **swing**. (I barely caught him!)

2. Referee **two** basketball and **three** volleyball games. (My cheeks were weak from whistling!)

3 Break up **four** fights, clean **five** skinned snouts, and put Band-Aids on **six** knees.

4 Place ice packs on **seven** lumps of various sizes and in various locations.

5 Dry the tears of eight little mice, and comfort **nine** mouselings with broken hearts. (I had to wring out my handkerchief after all those tears!)

And then Punk Rat challenged me to a race on the jungle gym. I was about to refuse, but suddenly Benjamin piped up.

"That's *baby stuff* for my uncle," Benjamin announced proudly. "He's not a wimp!"

After that statement, how could I say no? I climbed up the monkey bars and dove headfirst down the **tube** slide. All at once, I stopped. I was stuck! I was too big for the slide!

I felt so sorry for myself. It was definitively a BAD day.

"Would somebody please get me out!"

I yelled.

DEFINITELY A BAD DAY!

WHAT ARE YOU DOING HERE?

Luckily, Henry Handipaws came to **MY RESCUE** again. "Mr. Stilton, you've got yourself in a tight squeeze!" he said. He yanked me right out. What a close call! Henry patted me on the back and went on his way. Then I took the class back inside.

When we got to the classroom, Miss Angel Paws greeted me with a smile. She asked everyone to take a seat to listen to the next guest: the very famouse actor **Robert Rodentford**.

I rolled my eyes. I was sure he'd talk about his blockbuster movies and his yacht and all the beautiful rodents who are in love with him. In other words, I had a *preconceived** idea that he was a *snobby* and *silly* mouse.

I was wrong. He was much more than a *handsome snout*!

Robert Rodentford talked about the volunteer work he does to help save the **environment**. In fact, he never talked about himself. He discussed all the ways a rodent can **help** protect the earth.

I knew immediately that we would be **fast friends**. We were very different, but we both cared about the same things.

I was very interested in what he had to say, but then I **SAW** something slink by me. Sure enough, it was that sneaky, scaly class pet— *Spike*!

---

* To *preconceive* is to form an opinion (that may not be correct) about something or someone before having all the facts.

ROBERT RODENTFORD'S WORK TO SAVE THE ENVIRONMENT.

Robert Rodentford arrives to help after an oil tanker sinks and endangers penguins.

Rodentford squeaks out about smog, the dark truth about a growing pollution problem on Mouse Island.

Rodentford helps sandbag city dams when there is a flood emergency in New Mousiana.

Rodentford is down in the dumps about trash troubles.

My entire family had begged me not to get into any **trouble**, not to make a **fool** of myself, and not to disappoint Benjamin.

But that pesky gecko had gotten loose on my watch, and I felt responsible!

I looked at Spike, and he seemed to be smirking at me. A second later, he scurried across the room.

Then he climbed the wall and slipped into the air-conditioning duct!

I decided to follow him. I just *had* to **catch him**! I had to do it for Benjamin.

So, I pulled myself into the dark duct. I followed Spike along the narrow PASSAGEWAY, above classrooms, under the gym, and into the basement, until

he headed out into the hallway. I was still on my paws and knees when I bumped into her: a classy, *refined* rodent with her fur pulled into a neat bun.

I LOOKED at her, and she LOOKED at me.

We both yelled at the same time:

"What are you doing here?"

She had changed so much, but I knew it was her right away. How could I have forgotten her?

It was *Veronica Stiffwhiskers,* my greatest rival during my school days! This

was the mouse who had been so cute, so perfect, and so great at everything!

It had been her voice on the loudspeaker! She was now the **principal** of the school!

I was dumbfounded. I was trying to think of something *intelligent* to say when Spike scurried into an air-conditioning vent again.

THEN

NOW

I mumbled a silly excuse and dove in after Spike.

I always made a fool of myself in front of Veronica.

As I was scampering after Spike in the duct, I thought, *I'm sure she thinks I grew up to be a big fool. Sigh!*

WHERE DID THAT PESKY GECKO GO?

An (Almost) Olympic Performance

SPIKE!

ravenous cat.

the belly of a

was as dark as

long duct, which

Yoohoo!

fumbled down the

On all fours, I

I followed Spike **UP** and **down**, left and right, smacking my head against the low ceiling with every turn. Smack!

Spike made a quick turn and was about to slip into a new grate.

I **lunged** forward and pounced on him. All at once, I heard a creaking sound,

I fell, fell, fell, fell, fell, fell, fell fell, fell, fell, fell, fell, fell, fell, fell, fell, fell, fell, fell, fell, down!

I made a triple somersault with an elegant twist, landing on my feet with **slightly bent** knees. My gymnastic form was perfect! I didn't do it on purpose. In fact, if I had tried to do it, there was no way I could have performed so well. It was an (almost) **OLYMPiC** performance! But, of course, the one time I showed some agility and athletic ability, there was no one there to see me! Today had been full of so many blunders, I would have loved it if someone had seen my one **shining** moment!

As I was thinking this, a floodlight blinded me and thunderous **applause** shook the walls. A chorus of voices yelled:

"HOORAY FOR GERONIMO!"

STILTON, GERONIMO STILTON!

I was shocked!

Were they really all shouting my name?

"**Ge-ro-ni-mo!** Ge-ro-ni-mo! Ge-ro-ni-mo! Ge-ro-ni-mo!"

Was that *my* name on posters, programs, and banners?

I *RUBBED* my eyes. Maybe I had hit my head one too many times today. Maybe I had fainted.

I looked again. It was **real**. Everything was real. I wasn't dreaming. Holey cheese!

All these people were here for me. Veronica Stiffwhiskers came toward me with a huge smile. My, how she had changed!

"Today, on our school's Career Day, we want to honor our most **famouse** graduate. He's a wonderful example of how great achievement is possible through working hard every day and really *loving* what you do. He's won a Ratitzer Prize for his scoop on *The Curse of the Cheese Pyramid*, and he is a **bestselling** writer. His name is Stilton, *Geronimo Stilton*!"

Thunderous applause erupted around me.

Among the CHEERING audience, I saw my family standing to the side. No one was missing. Benjamin, Thea, Trap, Grandfather William, Tina Spicytail, Aunt Sweetfur . . . all of the *Stiltons* were there.

And there was Petunia Pretty Paws!

The principal's voice shook me back to reality.

". . . and to properly honor Little Tails Academy's most famouse graduate, who is also a dear old friend, I'd like to present him with a PLAQUE to remember this day."

While the photographers were shooting a million PHOTOS and the flashes were blinding me, she handed me a beautiful plaque engraved with my name.

"And if *Geronimo Stilton* doesn't mind, we'd like to keep the plaque in the school's lobby. It would be an honor to **SHOW** it in our trophy case, next to the **medals**, plaques, and *trophies* that our students have won."

Then she winked at me.

My, how she had changed!

PHOTOS AND AUTOGRAPHS

SO MANY PHOTOGRAPHERS!

HELP! THE FLASHES ARE BLINDING ME!

MORE PHOTOS! HOW EMBARRASSING!

HERE'S MY AUTOGRAPH!

WHAT AN HONOR!

Geronimo Stilton

THANK YOU, EVERYONE.
I'M VERY TOUCHED!

THE BEST NIBBLES FOR CHEESE-LOVING MICE!

Once the ceremony was over, the principal invited us to the dining hall. A **fabumouse buffet** had been set up, and there were countless cheesy delicacies!

There was a plate of Lulu's famous **triple-decker cheese** sandwiches, along with

many other amazing snacks: **FONDUE**, blue cheese **mousse** tarts, mozzarella and **cheddar cheese**, cheese shish-kabobs, and Swiss cheese souffle. Lulu had organized the buffet and, I can assure you, I have never seen more scrumptious, divine, original, whisker-licking delicacies in my life!

In other words, they were TOP-NOTCH nibbles for cheese-loving mice! It was then that I remembered that I hadn't eaten

breakfast or lunch. I was absolutely famished!

I was about to throw myself at the buffet when someone tapped me on the shoulder.

TAP, TAP!

I turned and saw a long, long line of rodents of every age waiting to congratulate me. I put down my sandwich with a sigh and turned toward them. I realized I would be skipping yet another meal. When I saw the first rodent on line was Henry Handipaws, I forgot my ravenous hunger.

"Thanks to you, I didn't make a complete fool of myself today," I told him warmly.

Suddenly, another rodent jumped out from behind him. They were almost **IDENTICAL**!

"Geronimo Stilton, you never change," the second mouse exclaimed. "You still get into such **trouble**!"

I stared at both of them, dumbfounded.

The second mouse's **whiskers** were **GRAYER**, he wasn't wearing a uniform, and he had a bit of a **tummy**, but otherwise the two mice almost looked like mirror images!

It was the legendary **Havarti Handipaws**. He had been the custodian during my time at Little Tails Academy. Back then, he helped me get out of tight squeezes a million times a day!

Henry Handipaws smiled.

Is that really you?

I'm Havarti Handipaws!

"*Like father, like son!*" he said. "Now you know why I knew so much about you, Mr. Stilton. My father told so many stories about you, and I decided to do the same kind of work as my father. I wanted to help a lot of shy little mice have more **confidence** in themselves."

I *thanked* them both from the bottom of my heart and spent the rest of the afternoon shaking hands, *smiling*, and signing autographs.

After a half hour, my paw was **weak** from all the handshakes. After an hour, my cheeks were *numb* from smiling so much. And after two hours, my shoulders were **bruised** from all the slaps and pats on the back!

But I was happy. Very, very happy.

I was actually ecstatic!

NOW I'M
IN THERE, TOO!

Even Grandfather William congratulated me. He slapped me on the shoulder the hardest!

"**Good for you**, Grandson!" he bellowed as I staggered from the blow to my shoulder. "This time you seemed like an upstanding mouse."

Trap threw a **spitball** in my ear.

"Nice going, Cousin," he said. "You looked less of a *fool* than usual. Except when you fell from the ceiling, that is!"

Aunt Sweetfur was *worried* about me. "You're pale," she whispered. "Didn't you eat enough?"

She placed a sweet little cheese tart in my paw. I stuffed it in my mouth before somebody could prevent me from tasting that little bit of heaven. It was **DEEELICIOUS**!

Robert Rodentford, Professor Sandsnout, Lulu Soufflé, Professor Magmamouse, and many other friends came over to congratulate me.

My friend Petunia Pretty Paws came over to give me a *tiny kiss* on the tip of my whiskers.

"I'm proud of you, Geronimo!" she said.

I was so embarrassed, I turned as **RED** as a tomato. Luckily, Benjamin came to give me a high five that almost took off my paw!

"You're awesome, Uncle Geronimo!" he exclaimed.

Behind him were all his school friends. Antonia had Spike in her arms.

"HOORAY FOR GERONIMO!" they all **YELLED** at once. "Hip,

hip, hooray for Spike's hero!"

"Tell me, Geronimo, did you like the surprise?" Veronica Stiffwhiskers asked. Then she turned to the mouselings.

"Hurry, everyone head to the lobby," she instructed them. "We have one more very **IMPORTANT** thing we need to do!"

The mouselings happily accompanied me

to the lobby. Veronica winked at me as she opened the trophy case.

"This time, you **win**!" she said. "You're our most famouse graduate."

She placed the plaque with my name on it inside the case.

"THANK YOU!" I shouted happily.

"Now I'm in there, too!"

Want to read my next adventure? I can't wait to tell you all about it!

SINGING SENSATION

When my friend Champ Strongpaws entered me in the New Mouse City Song Festival, I couldn't believe it. Me, a singer? I can't squeak a single note! I could tell I was in for an enormouse adventure!

And don't miss any of my other fabumouse adventures!

#1 LOST TREASURE OF THE EMERALD EYE

#2 THE CURSE OF THE CHEESE PYRAMID

#3 CAT AND MOUSE IN A HAUNTED HOUSE

#4 I'M TOO FOND OF MY FUR!

#5 FOUR MICE DEEP IN THE JUNGLE

#6 PAWS OFF, CHEDDARFACE!

#7 RED PIZZAS FOR A BLUE COUNT

#8 ATTACK OF THE BANDIT CATS

#9 A FABUMOUSE VACATION FOR GERONIMO

#10 ALL BECAUSE OF A CUP OF COFFEE

#11 IT'S HALLOWEEN, YOU 'FRAIDY MOUSE!

#12 MERRY CHRISTMAS, GERONIMO!

#13 THE PHANTOM OF THE SUBWAY

#14 THE TEMPLE OF THE RUBY OF FIRE

#15 THE MONA MOUSA CODE

#16 A CHEESE-COLORED CAMPER

#17 WATCH YOUR WHISKERS, STILTON!

#18 SHIPWRECK ON THE PIRATE ISLANDS

#19 MY NAME IS STILTON, GERONIMO STILTON

#20 SURF'S UP, GERONIMO!

#21 THE WILD, WILD WEST

#22 THE SECRET OF CACKLEFUR CASTLE

A CHRISTMAS TALE

#23 VALENTINE'S DAY DISASTER

#24 FIELD TRIP TO NIAGARA FALLS

#25 THE SEARCH FOR SUNKEN TREASURE

#26 THE MUMMY WITH NO NAME

#27 THE CHRISTMAS TOY FACTORY

#28 WEDDING CRASHER

#29 DOWN AND OUT DOWN UNDER

#30 THE MOUSE ISLAND MARATHON

#31 THE MYSTERIOUS CHEESE THIEF

CHRISTMAS CATASTROPHE

#32 VALLEY OF THE GIANT SKELETONS

#33 GERONIMO AND THE GOLD MEDAL MYSTERY

#34 GERONIMO STILTON, SECRET AGENT

#35 A VERY MERRY CHRISTMAS

#36 GERONIMO'S VALENTINE

#37 THE RACE ACROSS AMERICA

THEA STILTON AND THE DRAGON'S CODE

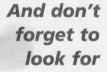
And don't forget to look for

#39 SINGING SENSATION

THEA STILTON AND THE MOUNTAIN OF FIRE

ABOUT THE AUTHOR

Born in New Mouse City, Mouse Island, Geronimo Stilton is Rattus Emeritus of Mousomorphic Literature and of Neo-Ratonic Comparative Philosophy. For the past twenty years, he has been running *The Rodent's Gazette,* New Mouse City's most widely read daily newspaper.

Stilton was awarded the Ratitzer Prize for his scoops on *The Curse of the Cheese Pyramid* and *The Search for Sunken Treasure.* He has also received the Andersen 2000 Prize for Personality of the Year. One of his bestsellers won the 2002 eBook Award for world's best ratlings' electronic book. His works have been published all over the globe.

In his spare time, Mr. Stilton collects antique cheese rinds and plays golf. But what he most enjoys is telling stories to his nephew Benjamin.

THE RODENT'S GAZETTE

1. Main entrance
2. Printing presses (where the books and newspaper are printed)
3. Accounts department
4. Editorial room (where the editors, illustrators, and designers work)
5. Geronimo Stilton's office
6. Storage space for Geronimo's books

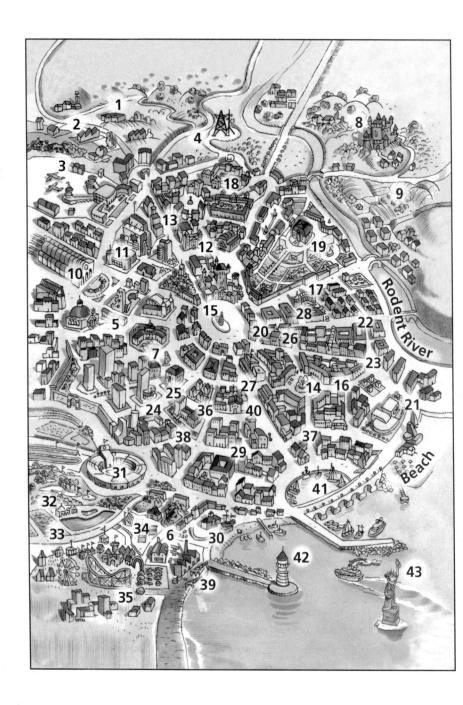

Map of New Mouse City

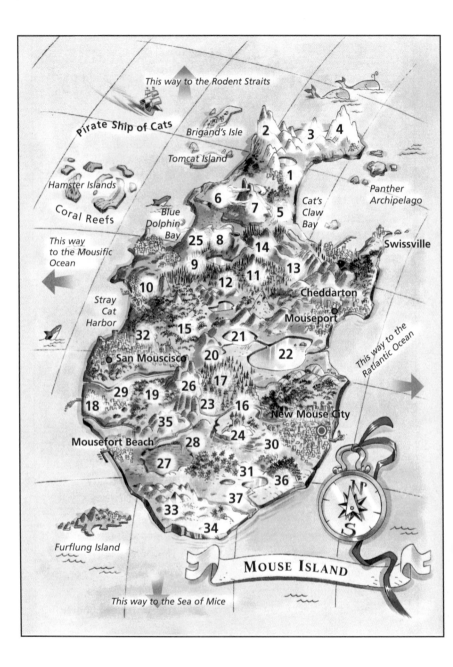

This way to the Rodent Straits

Pirate Ship of Cats

Brigand's Isle

Tomcat Island

Hamster Islands

Coral Reefs

Blue Dolphin Bay

This way to the Mousific Ocean

Stray Cat Harbor

San Mouscisco

Panther Archipelago

Cat's Claw Bay

Swissville

Cheddarton

Mouseport

This way to the Ratlantic Ocean

New Mouse City

Mousefort Beach

Furflung Island

MOUSE ISLAND

This way to the Sea of Mice

Map of Mouse Island

1. Big Ice Lake
2. Frozen Fur Peak
3. Slipperyslopes Glacier
4. Coldcreeps Peak
5. Ratzikistan
6. Transratania
7. Mount Vamp
8. Roastedrat Volcano
9. Brimstone Lake
10. Poopedcat Pass
11. Stinko Peak
12. Dark Forest
13. Vain Vampires Valley
14. Goose Bumps Gorge
15. The Shadow Line Pass
16. Penny Pincher Castle
17. Nature Reserve Park
18. Las Ratayas Marinas
19. Fossil Forest
20. Lake Lake
21. Lake Lakelake
22. Lake Lakelakelake
23. Cheddar Crag
24. Cannycat Castle
25. Valley of the Giant Sequoia
26. Cheddar Springs
27. Sulfurous Swamp
28. Old Reliable Geyser
29. Vole Vale
30. Ravingrat Ravine
31. Gnat Marshes
32. Munster Highlands
33. Mousehara Desert
34. Oasis of the Sweaty Camel
35. Cabbagehead Hill
36. Rattytrap Jungle
37. Rio Mosquito

Dear mouse friends,
Thanks for reading, and farewell
till the next book.
It'll be another whisker-licking-good
adventure, and that's a promise!

Geronimo Stilton

great. But I didn't trust McDonald's question. I thought perhaps he was trying to get me out of the way because he knew I wanted to manage and I represented a threat to the job security of Joe Frazier, his hand-picked manager at the time.

"I don't know," I said. "I don't want to go if it keeps me from coming back here and managing the team someday. I'd like to talk to Mr. Grant."

M. Donald Grant was running the Mets in those days. I met with him in the manager's office. I told him, "Look, you don't need my permission to trade me to the Yankees, but if it's going to keep me from being considered here as a manager, I'd rather not go." Grant thanked me, and they didn't trade me.

In May of the next season, 1977, we were playing an exhibition game against our Triple-A team, Tidewater, in Virginia. I didn't play, and was shaving in the clubhouse before the end of the game to expedite our quick getaway. In the mirror I saw McDonald walking up behind me. Oh, shit, I thought. He's going to get on me about shaving during the game. Instead McDonald said, "How would you like to manage this team?"

"Yeah, I would," I said.

"Tomorrow meet Mr. Grant at his apartment in Manhattan at nine o'clock in the morning."

After McDonald left, Tom Seaver walked out from a bathroom stall. He had heard the whole conversation. He didn't say a word to me. He just raised his eyebrows as if to say, "Wow," and never mentioned it again. The Mets traveled to Philadelphia after that game, whereupon I rented a car and drove home to New Jersey so that I could meet Grant in the morning. Grant made it clear to me at the meeting that he wanted me to replace Frazier, though he had not decided on the timing of the move. I drove back to Philadelphia and had lunch with my friend McCarver, who was playing for the Phillies. I told him about the managing offer. He was very happy for me. I really liked Frazier as a person, but I had trouble playing for him because he didn't have a lot of confidence in my ability. When I got to the ballpark that night, Frazier called me into his office.

"We checked for curfew last night, Joe," he said. "You weren't in your room."

I felt terribly uncomfortable. Here was a guy who was going to lose his job to me, and I knew it and he didn't. It was horrible.

"I had to go home," I told Frazier.

"Why didn't you ask me?" he said.

"Well, if I asked you and you said no, I had to go home anyway," I said. "And then it would have been insubordination. So I took my chances. I'll pay whatever fine you think is right."

"No, there's no fine," Frazier said. "Just don't do it again."

One week later, on May 31, 1977, the Mets named me manager. I remained on the active playing roster for about three weeks before I decided to devote all my time to managing. My energy and my outlook were completely rejuvenated by becoming a manager. The best job in baseball is playing every day. The next best job in baseball is managing—it easily beats playing part time. I wasn't nervous at all about managing, even though I had never done it before (although Gibson used to accuse me of doing it all the time with the Cardinals). My excitement was equal to being called up to the big leagues for the first time. I won my first game and eleven of my first sixteen, but again my timing was terrible. Sixteen days into my first managing job, the Mets shook up the team with what became known as the Midnight Massacre, the symbolic beginning of one of the Mets' most inept eras. Just before the June 15 trading deadline, they traded Seaver, who had been feuding with Grant over his contract, to the Reds; Dave Kingman, our best power hitter, to the Padres; and infielder Mike Phillips to the Cardinals. We finished 64-98, the first of four straight seasons in which we lost at least 95 games—a streak broken only by the 1981 players' strike.

The World Series? That was as far away as the moon. In those years I set my sights on much smaller goals. Winning two out of three games against the Dodgers practically made our season. My bad timing was easy to rationalize in this case: If the Mets had been more committed to winning, they would have hired a more experienced manager. They needed a popular figure in New York and someone who was adept at handling the media during that time of transition.

We may have been an awful club, but we had our share of fun. I had some colorful characters on those teams, such as Willie Montanez. One day he got upset when I sent Joel Youngblood to pinch-run for him. He was so mad, he challenged Youngblood to a race in the outfield after the game. They ran a dead heat. Montanez couldn't wait to tell me about it. "Great," I said. "If you ran hard like that all the time, I wouldn't have to pinch-run for you."

In 1979 we had Richie Hebner at third base. Richie used to tell us stories about his off-season job: He worked for his father digging graves in Massachusetts. One time his father complained that Richie wasn't digging the graves deep enough. Richie told him, "Ain't none of them crawled out yet."

We also had a confident kid from Brooklyn named Lee Mazzilli. After the 1979 season the Mets gave him a three-year contract, even though he wasn't close to being a free agent. He came up to me and said, "Listen, Joe, if there's anything I can do for you, with the front office or whatever about a contract extension, just let me know." When players felt so secure, because of their contracts, that they were giving advice to managers, that's when I knew that big money was starting to make a mess out of the traditional order of the game. When I first joined the union, our big concerns had been things like getting better shower nozzles and squeezing another couple of bucks of meal money out of the owners. The union eventually grew so powerful that it created a monster.

In 1980 Fred Wilpon and Nelson Doubleday bought the Mets and hired Frank Cashen to be their general manager. That June they held the first pick of the amateur draft. Darryl Strawberry looked like the most talented player available. The Mets briefly toyed with the idea of not drafting him. They were a little afraid of stories that Darryl had gotten into some trouble in high school, like missing practices. They had another player in mind, Billy Beane, and asked my opinion. "You've got to take the best player available and worry about the other stuff later," I said. They drafted Darryl and wound up getting Beane in the second round. I met Darryl at Dodger Stadium in Los Angeles soon after the draft, and we joked about him playing for me someday soon. It took sixteen years and a lifetime of trouble for Darryl, but we finally found ourselves on the same team with the Yankees, in 1996.

I had two astute pitching coaches with the Mets, Rube Walker and Bob Gibson. Rube taught me that you can't win without good pitching—baseball is the only sport where you can't run out the clock by freezing the ball. You need twenty-seven outs and the pitcher's involved in every one of them. Gibby had tremendous knowledge to give pitchers but was willing to share it only with people who sincerely wanted to listen. A lot of pitchers don't think they need help, and Bob was turned off by those types and wouldn't hesitate to show them his gruff side.

Cashen thought I was too soft as a manager. That was a rap that followed me for a long time: that I was too much of a "player's manager." But I wasn't any different as manager of the world champion Yankees than I had been with the last place Mets. In fact, I was probably more of a player's manager with the Yankees. I was always hanging out in the clubhouse before and after games. That's what made 1996 so sweet for me. It's nice to know you can be all those things people thought of as negative and still win. I've always believed you can make your point without throwing food across the room or embarrassing people in the newspapers. I'm very proud that I never tried to make myself look good by blaming somebody else.

Though Cashen considered me too laid back, the biggest disagreement I had with him happened over an episode when he thought I was too tough on my players. When I took over as manager of the Mets, I permitted the players to drink at the hotel bars on the road. Too many players took that as a mandate. My coaches and I practically had to drag guys out of the bars at closing time, so we changed the rule and prohibited players from hotel bars. That's always been my approach: I give players privileges, and if they abuse them, I take them away. One late night in Montreal in 1981, I walked into the hotel bar as I came back from dinner with my coaches. I saw Ron Hodges, a catcher, and Dyar

The year is 1962, and I am with Stan Musial in the old Busch Stadium.

On the field with my son Michael and Willie Mays.

Sitting with a friend in my first car, a 1960 Thunderbird that I bought from an unassuming Milwaukee car salesman named Bud Selig.

Frank and I at the Milwaukee Writers' Dinner in 1962 celebrating my rookie of the year award with the Braves.

At the 1965 all-star game in Minnesota, with Willie Stargell and Willie Mays. We all hit home runs that game. I also caught all nine innings. (UPI)

At the all-star game in St. Louis in 1966. The signature says: "To Joe, a great hitter. Best always, Ted Williams." (*NEWS DEMOCRAT*)

Accepting the 1971 MVP award and batting championship award in 1972 from National League President Chub Feeney.

Honored in February 1972 for the MVP award alongside Sandy Koufax.

Spring training, 1972, in St. Petersburg, Florida. Behind me, doing sit-ups, is Stan Musial, who liked to work out with the club even after he retired.

The most courageous ballplayer I've ever known—Bob Gibson. Shea Stadium, 1973: Gibson had blown his knee out the top half of the inning before, running the bases, but he still tried to pitch. He collapsed after releasing the ball. After his recovery he came back to pitch again.

Me, Gibson, and Tim McCarver in 1974. Because Gibson was pitching that day and wore his trademark game-face scowl, he refused to have his picture taken. We convinced him his back would do, so he agreed.

July 16, 1977, one of my favorite photographs: in the dugout at Shea Stadium for an Old-Timers' Day Game with Mickey Mantle, Ralph Kiner, and Joe DiMaggio. (LOUIS REQUENA)

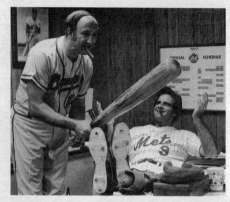

With my brother Frank in my office as the Mets manager in 1977. (AP/WIDE WORLD PHOTOS)

At another Old-Timers' Day game with Frank.

My fiftieth birthday party, July 18, 1990, with Rocco and Frank. That day I had a conversation with the St. Louis Cardinals about the possibility of managing them.

October 1982: in the dugout talking to the press as the manager for the Braves in the playoffs against St. Louis. (HERREN)

With George Kissell and Mike Shannon in San Diego. I learned more about the game of baseball from Kissell than from anyone else.

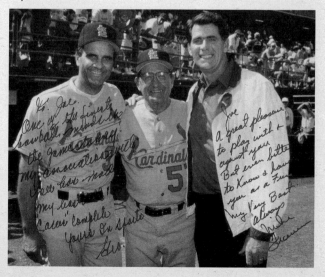

Interviewing Roger Clemens. I was an announcer for six years, from 1985 to 1990.

December 14, 1995: in the hospital, holding Andrea Rae for the first time.

Making a point with President Bush at Dodger Stadium.

Miller, a pitcher, drinking beer in there. I sent one of my coaches, Chuck Cottier, to tell them to drink up and get out. They refused. I did all I could to keep Gibby from pulverizing those guys right there.

That was one of the toughest nights I've ever had as a manager. I had to decide how to punish them. They were guilty of insubordination. The next day I decided to suspend them and sent them back to New York, while the rest of the team traveled to Philadelphia for a series against the Phillies. It wasn't long before I got a call from Cashen.

"Don't you realize that this whole incident is over just one beer?" he said.

"Yep, I sure do," I told him.

"Well," Frank said, "if you reconsider and lift the suspension, I can have them in Philadelphia in time for the game tonight."

"Frank," I said, "if we do that, we might as well take all the rules and shove them up your ass."

As a manager, you can have all the rules you want, but you have to have the right people to make them work. That's one of the reasons why we won with the Yankees. We didn't have players who wanted to test me. They understood the team concept. John Wetteland was the most honest guy I've ever managed. He would fine himself over infractions I knew nothing about. He would walk into my office every once in a while and throw money on my desk. "What's that for?" I'd ask. He'd say something like "I was late for stretching exercises."

Jimmy Leyritz would push the envelope with me—he liked to be thirty seconds late a lot—but it was nothing close to insubordination. And every once in a while I'd have to chew out the players hanging out in the clubhouse during games. Some guys liked to go back there to stretch or hit into a net, but every once in a while it was ridiculously crowded back there. I'd be into the game and all of a sudden I'd look at the bench, and there would be only two guys there. I'd tell them later, "If we ever had a fight on the field, we'd get our asses kicked. At least assign yourselves numbers so you can go back during different innings."

Cashen fired me after that 1981 season, though it wasn't because of that disciplinary incident. Doubleday, Wilpon, and Cashen had given me a two-year contract going into that year, but I considered it more of a nice gesture, like a golden parachute, than a firm commitment, because new owners and new general managers don't like inheriting somebody else's manager. I wasn't bitter about being fired. Look at my record: 286-420. The fact that I lasted five seasons in New York with that record may have been my greatest accomplishment in baseball.

The 1981 season was a miserable one. Not only did I get fired, but a strike by the players wiped out almost one-third of the season, and my marriage to Dani got so bad that I finally moved out. I'm not sure why I stuck it out so long with her. Maybe it was because divorce meant another failure. And for a long time I believed I could make things right. I tried to open up more and pay more attention to her, but she seemed to think it was too late. That was when I felt like we had hit a brick wall. But there was one night in that otherwise awful season that turned my life around. Gibby, myself, and some of my other coaches were sitting in a hotel bar in Cincinnati after dinner on August 23. It was a Sunday. The place was dead, and I nearly was too. I was in no mood to meet anybody. I was sipping a glass of sparkling water. And then I saw this tall slender waitress. She was reading a book—that's how slow the place was. She was striking. I said out loud, "Wow. Would you look at her."

"Go over and introduce yourself, Joe," Gibby said.

"Nah," I said. I really wasn't in the mood for it.

"Then I'll go talk to her for you," said Gibby, and he walked over and told her that I wanted to meet her.

She came over to our table, and we hit it off right away. I learned that her name was Alice and that she was a few days away from her twenty-fourth birthday. I was forty-one. Gibby said, "Why don't you ask her to lunch tomorrow?" So I did. She accepted. The next time August 23 fell on a Sunday—six years later—we were married. I fell in love pretty quickly with Ali. She was very easy to talk with right from the start, probably because she grew up with fifteen brothers and sisters. I was relaxed around her. That was so important for me, because up until I met Ali, home was never a comfortable place. Home to me had been a place of fear, because of my father, and then a place of tension, because of my two failed marriages.

When the Mets fired me, they also fired Gibson. He took it much harder than I did. Gibby had played with one club, the Cardinals, his whole career and was a Hall of Famer. The rejection devastated him. He was so burned by the experience that when I later asked him to coach for me with the Braves, he said he wouldn't come unless they gave him the security of a two-year deal, an unusual contract for a coach. He got it.

Unlike Bob, I had been traded twice before, so I was somewhat accustomed to that empty feeling of rejection. It didn't last long, though, because two weeks later I interviewed for the managing jobs in San Diego (the Padres hired Dick Williams) and Atlanta. John Mullen, the Braves' general manager, interviewed me in Atlanta. We agreed on a three-year contract with an attendance clause. A few days later I was awakened by a telephone call from Ted Turner, the America's Cup yachtsman, CNN founder, and colorful Braves' owner whom the press liked to call "the Mouth of the South."

"You drive a hard bargain," Ted said.

"Yeah," I said. "Is it a deal?"

"Yeah," Ted said.

A little while later John Mullen told me, "You weren't my choice, but let's work together the best we can." I didn't like the sound of that. I also found out later from Ted that Mullen hadn't told Turner about the attendance clause. Ted said later he would not have agreed if he'd known about it, so he wouldn't put it into my contract. My tenure in Atlanta began on shaky footing. But when the 1982 season opened, I was as happy as I could be: I had a three-year contract, I was in love with a beautiful woman, and my team had started with thirteen straight wins. It was after our first five that we went to Cincinnati and I called Ali's parents, Lucille and Ed Wolterman, for the first time. I asked them if they wanted tickets to the game. They said no. I heard a lot of mistrust in their voices. Ali told me later that when she first told them she was dating the manager of the Braves, Ed, who was pretending to be sleeping on a couch, jumped up and said, "How the hell old is this guy?" I eventually won them over though. When I called them to ask for their daughter's hand in marriage, Ali's mother told her she had worn out three pairs of rosary beads praying for that day to come.

The first time I met Ali's parents was on the Braves' second trip to Cincinnati in 1982. I was more nervous about that than I was for the 1996 World Series. My palms were sweaty. I wanted to be so agreeable around her father that I said yes to everything he asked. "Do you want a sandwich?" Sure. "Do you want a beer?" Sure, though I never drank on the day of a game. "Do you want spaghetti and meatballs?" Sure. "Another beer?" Sure.

"Another beer?" Sure. By the time I left for the ballpark, I was both stuffed and tipsy.

That 13–0 start was incredible. We had so many comeback wins that during one game, which we were losing 5–0, Dale Murphy, our great center fielder, said to me, "Well, they got us where we want them." We had thin starting pitching that year, but we did have good arms in the bullpen and a lot of thunder in our lineup with Murphy, Chris Chambliss, who became my hitting coach with the Cardinals and Yankees, and Bob Horner. Bob had awesome talent, enough to hit .320 with 30 to 40 home runs every season. But he never got in very good shape, which caused him to get hurt. He'd always be looking to find reasons to come out of games. I knew about Horner's reputation, and I knew how important he was to us. So one of the first things I did as manager of the Braves was to name him captain of the team. Murph and Chambliss, both of whom were leaders, were much better suited for that role. So before I told Horner about it, I explained to Murph and Chambliss why I was doing it: I needed Bob to be more responsible. Being true professionals, they understood and never beefed. Bob had a good year for me, batting .261 with 32 home runs and 97 runs batted in, despite missing twenty-two games with an injury.

I never seriously considered naming a captain on the Yankees. One of the big stories in spring training regarded how we were going to replace Don Mattingly, the former captain, and his leadership. If

I had picked a new captain, I might as well have drawn a bull's-eye on his back—that person would have been inundated with questions about replacing Mattingly. I told reporters that people like Joe Girardi, David Cone, Paul O'Neill, and Wade Boggs all had leadership qualities. Some people in the front office, though, insisted that we at least needed to select someone who would lead the team on the field at the start of every game, a responsibility that belonged to Mattingly. That's something I never would have thought about or considered important, but I was told we had to have someone do it. So I said it might as well be Boggs, an everyday player with the most experience.

After Captain Horner and the rest of my Braves posted our twelfth straight win, which set a modern major league record at the start of a season, the fans ran on the field as if we had won the pennant. We won again the next night. In our fourteenth game we had a thousand different ways to win, but we lost. We lost four more in a row after that. We were up and down all year. After that 13-0 start we went 76–73 the rest of the season, including one stretch where we were 2–19. We took a one-game lead over the Dodgers into the last day. We were playing the Padres in San Diego, and the Dodgers were playing in San Francisco against the Giants. Before our game Turner walked into the clubhouse.

After some friendly greetings I said to Ted, "You know, Ted, I was just telling Gibby that I wish I could give him the ball to pitch this game."

Turner looked at Gibson and said, "You think you could?" He was ready to sign my forty-six-year-old pitching coach to a contract. As it turned out, maybe I should have started Gibby. We got our ass kicked. The Padres jumped out to a big lead. As our game wore on, we knew we needed help from the Giants. If they beat the Dodgers, we would be West Division champions. If the Dodgers won, we would have to play them in a one-game playoff the next day. Toward the end of the game one of my players, Jerry Royster, grounded out and then came running back to the dugout at full speed with a smile on his face.

"Joe Morgan just hit a three-run home run!" he said. Jerry was talking about the game in San Francisco. The Giants were winning. He explained that the Padres' catcher, Terry Kennedy, had told him about it while he was batting. Kennedy got the information from the Padres' dugout, where one of the San Diego coaches, Whitey Wietelman, had a radio. We hurried through the rest of our game in time to watch the last inning of the Dodgers' loss on television. We were West Division champions. It would have been much more fun to win our game and celebrate on the field, but no one in our clubhouse was complaining. The Braves had not been to the postseason since 1969. We'd take it any way we could get it.

That was my best shot at the World Series until 1996. We needed three wins against St. Louis in the National League Championship Series to get there. We started off with a 1–0 lead in Game One with my ace pitcher, Phil Niekro, on the mound. And then it rained and the game was called off. We lost three straight games after that. The Cardinals simply were a better team than us. We were overmatched.

I lasted only two more years with the Braves, even though we finished in second place both times. Ted and I just never had a relationship built on trust. After we won our division title, for instance, I was still so angry about Ted's refusal to honor the attendance clause that I tried to stop the release of our television movie, because they weren't paying me. Turner's TV people had hooked me up to a microphone for every game that season to record all my dugout conversations, arguments with umpires, and meetings with pitchers on the mound. The recordings became the centerpiece to the movie. Another time, in 1983, Ted second-guessed me about some moves I had made in a losing game the previous night. He was screaming wildly at me in a conference room adjacent to his office in front of other people from the Braves' front office. I was humiliated. We won the game that afternoon, and Ted came into the clubhouse with a big smile. I asked him to come into my office and I closed the door behind him.

"Ted," I said, "you can fire me or do anything you want with me. I respect you. You're the owner. And if I worried about being second-guessed, we never would have won last year. But don't you ever,

ever yell at me in front of a bunch of people again. You can yell at me all you want—just come in this office and scream. Don't do it in front of an audience."

Ted got the message. Steinbrenner gets a lot of notoriety for aggravating his managers, but George isn't nearly as meddlesome as Ted was in those days. Working for Steinbrenner has been a walk in the park compared with working for Turner. Once the 1996 season started, I didn't hear from Steinbrenner until four weeks into the regular season—and that was only because I called him up to ask about one of his horses that was running in the Kentucky Derby. I called him April 29 as our team bus was driving to Baltimore for a series against the Orioles. "George," I told him, "I've heard all these horror stories about you bugging your manager, and I had to call you." George laughed. At least he doesn't like to hang out in the clubhouse the way Turner did. Ted wanted to be loved by the players more than anything. The players came first, and then his staff. He had a habit after the last out of jumping over the wall of the stands and running through our dugout to the clubhouse. One night he ran from the stands into the dugout, and I had to tell him, "Uh, Ted, that's only two outs." And he ran all the way back and jumped back into his seat.

I liked Ted. We just never hit it off. He took me to his plantation in South Carolina after the 1983 season to talk to me about my contract. (He actually added two seasons to it, extending it through

1986.) He gave me a rifle and made sure I was in front of him when I was carrying it. After a long walk through the woods, he sent me up a tree to shoot deer. I saw one deer but didn't dare pull the trigger. The next day we got up at four in the morning to go duck hunting. All I could think about was getting back to sleep. I was a kid from Brooklyn. About the closest I had ever been to that kind of country life was chasing batting-practice balls on the swampy field of Waycross, Georgia. What did I know or care about that stuff?

Toward the end of the 1984 season I started picking up signals that the Braves were going to fire me. If you hang around baseball long enough, you can see it coming. I was making phone calls to the front office, and nobody was returning them. Nobody from upstairs was coming down to the clubhouse. It was like I had a contagious disease. Some people in the front office were quietly pushing Ted to hire Eddie Haas, a southern man who had been in the Atlanta organization for years. Finally I called Ted on the day after the season and said, "I want to come see you." I had a feeling I was going to be fired, and I wanted to make it easy for him. He invited me to his office. Sure enough, he told me I was fired. Ted looked a little uncomfortable doing it. He appeared relaxed whenever he was dealing with people in a large group. But in a one-on-one setting, he looked ill at ease. Being fired by him hurt me much more than being fired by the Mets. In New York the team had changed owners. I understood and expected that move. But in Atlanta it was political. It really bothered me.

A few weeks later I was watching television with Ali. Some celebrity was being interviewed. The person was asked, "How would you like to be remembered?" Ali turned to me and said, "That's a great question. What would you say, Joe?"

"I don't know," I said. "Just a guy who never realized his dream."

I was really down in the dumps. This time after I was fired, nobody called. So I picked up the phone and called the California Angels, when I heard from a New York sportswriter, Phil Pepe, about an opening there for a broadcaster. I sent them a tape of color commentary I had done for CBS radio with Jack Buck during the 1981 Division Series between Philadelphia and Montreal. Gene Autry, the old cowboy and Angels owner, hired me. I worked for five years with Bob Starr and then, in 1990, with Joe Garagiola and Reggie Jackson. I enjoyed the work, but I missed managing. I received slight interest about managerial openings with Houston and Pittsburgh in 1985, Minnesota in 1986, and Boston in 1988. Those jobs went to Hal Lanier, Jim Leyland, Tom Kelly, and Joe Morgan, respectively.

After about three years of broadcasting, I began to think, This is it. I'm finished with managing. I'll never get to the World Series. I heard rumors that people were afraid to hire me because I wanted more control over running a team than most managers. I heard rumors that teams were afraid of having Gibson as a pitching coach—people assumed we were a package—because of his intimidating personality. I don't know what it was, but I do know that to be hired as a manager, you need connections. And I had none. Actually, I did have one connection. My friend Dal Maxvill was the general manager of the Cardinals. But that didn't do me any good because his manager, Whitey Herzog, was a fixture in St. Louis. Then one day in July 1990 Maxvill called me. Herzog had tired of managing and quit. Maxvill needed a manager. He wanted to talk to me. I was on my way to Las Vegas to celebrate my fiftieth birthday. Maxie told me he'd meet me there at the Sands Hotel.

We sat for two and half hours in a back booth at the Sands coffee shop. I let Maxie know I was very interested. Ali encouraged me to do it. I had a comfortable job in the broadcast booth, and we liked living in California, but she knew how much my World Series dream meant to me. Maxie wanted me to manage right away, but the Angels were just about to start a three-city trip, and I didn't want to leave them short in the broadcast booth. Maxie and I agreed I would begin managing the Cardinals August 1. We also agreed that my contract would include the same rollover provision the Cardinals gave Herzog. The club would extend my contract before the close of each season so that I would never go into the next season as a lame duck manager. I was excited. I hadn't managed in six years. It was like getting my first job all over again.

It turned out that the Cardinals were entering a transitional period. Gussie Busch had died in 1989, leaving his son, August, in charge. August was a terrific businessman with the Anheuser-Busch brewery, but he had no passion for baseball. If something didn't fit into his bottom line, then it didn't make sense to him. He wasn't going to spend the necessary money on the baseball team to make it a contender. I think Whitey had seen that change coming when he quit. We had some decent teams in St. Louis when I was there, but we never made the necessary player acquisitions in the off-season or down the stretch to get us over the hump.

The Cardinals posted winning records in my first three full seasons managing. George Kissell was a tremendous help to me as my spring training coordinator. He held a yellow pad during the games and jotted down things he noticed about our club that needed attention. Then we would review his list of our mistakes. He'd give me advice on strategy and then say, "I'm just giving you the aspirin, Joe. You decide whether to swallow it or spit it out." Just as in my playing days with the Cardinals, he questioned everything. He had a favorite line: "Joe, who wrote the book?" And I'd say, "Nobody, George. Nobody wrote the book." That was George's way of reminding me that I could make any move I wanted as a manager as long as I had the right reasons for it—whether it was unpopular or unorthodox. That style helped me in the 1996 World Series. I surprised some people with moves like benching Wade Boggs against a right-handed pitcher, letting my pitcher bat in the ninth inning, and putting the potential winning run on base intentionally. But that's the way I've always managed. I'm more concerned about winning the game than trying to cover my butt.

When you don't get results with that kind of managing style, you look like a dummy. I looked real dumb in 1994, especially in a game in Houston on my birthday. July 18 has become a dreaded date for me. I can hardly remember ever getting a hit as a player on my birthday or a win as a manager. Ali had flown in to be with me on my birthday, but I wasn't such great company that night. The game in Houston was a catastrophe. We blew an 11–0 lead and lost 15–12. On top of that, I got up in the middle of the night to go to the bathroom and broke my toe on the end of the bed. The next day Stuart Meyer, the president of the club, gave me a public vote of confidence. I appreciated the sentiment, but the timing wasn't great after such a bad loss that had the radio talk shows in St. Louis calling for my head.

Two days later I was called by August Busch to a meeting at a building at a soccer park on the west side of the city, where Anheuser-Busch likes to hold corporate meetings. Stuart Meyer and Maxvill also were there. Maxie and I sat down and thought we were going to talk about the club's game plan for the next year. August started the meeting by saying to me, "There is not going to be any extension of your contract."

Maxie jumped in right away, saying, "I can't do this to this man. When he came over here, I told him he would never go into a season on the last year of a contract."

"Well, we're changing that around here," August said. Apparently the public humiliation of that loss in Houston and the odd timing of Meyer's backing of me reflected poorly on the brewery. August hated to see even a hint of embarrassment come to the family business.

I looked at Maxie, and I could see the veins bulging in his neck. He stood up.

"This is all about that fucking 11-0 game, isn't it?" Maxie yelled. "Why don't you just sell the club?"

Then August stood up and his veins started to bulge. "Don't you tell me what to do," he screamed.

The meeting lasted about fifteen minutes. When we left, Maxie and I had to check if we still had our clothes on—that's how badly we were undressed. On our way home we stopped for breakfast. Maxie said, "Joe, I think I got myself fired this morning." I said, "Well, you did what you think is right. That's most important."

About a week later the major league players walked out on strike. We happened to be in Florida at the time, one of fourteen clubs on the road. All of the thirteen other clubs flew their players back on charter flights to their home cities. The Cardinals told their players to find their own way home. My players were rightfully pissed about it. August Busch then replaced Meyer, who resigned, with Mark Lamping. One day Maxvill was supposed to fly to St. Petersburg to watch some of our minor leaguers play. Lamping asked him to change his flight to sometime later that day. He was just stringing him along; Lamping fired Maxvill before he ever made that later flight. I felt badly about that because Maxie had sealed his fate when he stuck his neck out for me at that meeting with August. He's a loyal guy, and I've always appreciated that quality in a person. Lamping never bothered to pick up the phone and call me after he was hired. He started calling some of the players instead. Finally I called him and told him I wanted to meet with him and Jerry Ritter, one of August Busch's top executives. "How can you talk to the players before you even talk to the manager?" I said at the meeting. "You might as well make it easy on the next general manager coming in here and fire me; give him a clean slate." I went to the ballpark and started cleaning out some of my stuff. Lamping saw me. "What are you doing?" he said. "You don't have to do that." I knew that in interviewing possible general managers—he eventually hired Walt Jocketty after also talking with Lee Thomas and Doug Melvin—Lamping spoke with Chris Chambliss about managing and also tried to get Jim Leyland from the Pirates. Once Jocketty was aboard,

I'm sure he made a run at getting Tony LaRussa. I was treated with no respect, and it bothered the hell out of me.

As the strike lingered on, the owners made plans to bring in replacement players. I wasn't around for the Black Sox scandal in 1919, but the travesty of replacement baseball in the spring of 1995 was the darkest time in the history of baseball, as far as I'm concerned. No baseball would have been much better than trying to force that inferior product on the public. I hated being around it, but I had signed a contract to manage the St. Louis Cardinals, no matter what players wore the uniform. As an old union man, I thought the players overreacted to the replacement player charade. Those guys weren't a threat to their jobs. If anything, the replacements reminded the whole world how talented and special the major leaguers are.

The owners were way off base in thinking the replacement idea would fly. One day in spring training I was in the restaurant at the Don Cesar hotel with Jocketty, Lamping, and Jerry Ritter. Our wives accompanied us. Jerry asked me, "What class of baseball do you think the replacements are equivalent to?" I said, "Low A ball." He looked at me in disbelief. He thought it was close to Triple-A baseball.

Then Lamping said, "It doesn't matter. By July the fans aren't going to really care who the players are on the field because all they want to do is come out to the ballpark, drink beer, and have fun with each other."

I looked at my wife, and she had to bite her lip. I was shocked myself. Here I was trying my whole life to win a championship, and this guy didn't even care who he sent out there in the uniform of the St. Louis Cardinals. I felt ashamed even to be associated with baseball management. August Busch also held a meeting with my staff and me about presenting a positive image to the press about replacement ball. Before the meeting I asked to talk with him privately. He was about to learn about the streak of honesty I shared with Rae. "I just want to tell you something," I said. "I will do anything you need me to do, but there's one thing I won't do: I won't lie. I can't lie and say I'm enjoying this or looking forward to this or whatever we're going to do. I can't do that. I'm telling you that now one-on-one so that you understand."

Then I told Busch that I had attended a union meeting in Orlando the previous night. I had gone there with some other managers, including Jim Fregosi, Gene Lamont, and Jim Leyland, to fight for my coaches because I heard the players were considering taking coaches off the list of people who get a cut of their licensing revenue. Busch was furious about me going there. I didn't give a shit if he fired me on the spot. He started talking again about the need to sell replacement baseball.

"I can't do that," I told him, "because eventually the major league players are going to be back."

"How do you know they'll be back?" he said.

Right then I really knew how screwed up the owners were. They actually believed that they could permanently replace the best players in the world with truck drivers, softball players, and a collection of has-been players. With the help of a court injunction, the major leaguers did come back in April—a lot quicker than August had thought. My relationship with them was irreparably damaged. I could tell they resented me for managing the replacement players. By June 16 we were in fourth place with a 20–27 record. Early in the morning we traded Todd Zeile to the Chicago Cubs. The deal wasn't supposed to be announced until one P.M., but I heard about it on the radio at about ten A.M. as I was driving home from getting a haircut. I called Walt Jocketty to tell him about it when I got home. He said, "Where are you?" I said, "I'm home." And he said, "I'll be right over." I hung up the phone and told Ali, "I think we're getting fired here." It was a strange feeling. I had never been fired during the season.

Walt came over, and he started crying. "We have to make a change," he said. "Don't worry about it, Walt," I said. I was the one getting fired, and there I was cheering *him* up. We talked for a while, then I gave him a bottle of wine and sent him on his way. I was sort of thankful he did fire me. It was bound to happen. It was like going to the dentist: Just get it over with. My first reaction was to want to curl up and hide. But then I told Ali, "Let's go out."

She said, "You want to go out to dinner?" I said, "Yeah, let's do it."

I wasn't ashamed of anything. There was no reason to hide. I had had a good run as a manager, and I planned to go back to broadcasting. The politics and players' attitudes in St. Louis had left a sour taste in my mouth anyway. I thought I was treated shabbily by the Cardinals, though I never said anything to embarrass the organization even when I was fired. I talked with Frank, and I could tell he was happy that I was finished with managing. He told me I didn't need the aggravation anymore. I couldn't argue with him.

I knew my window to getting to the World Series was not just closed, it had been slammed shut. I had been lucky enough to get managing jobs with all three of the teams I had played for—and been fired by every one of them. I had no more former teams left to come calling. Who would want a fifty-five-year-old manager who had been fired three times, had never been to the World Series, and had a lifetime record of more losses (1,003) than wins (894)? Nobody, I figured. By George, was I wrong.

CHAPTER 7

The Season of a Lifetime

AFTER I WAS FIRED ALI AND I moved to Cincinnati to be close to her family. In October, just before the Braves and Indians began the 1995 World Series, I took a trip to Las Vegas with one of my friends from Atlanta, Ed Maull. One day when I called home to talk to Ali, she said, "Joe Molloy and Gene Michael are trying to get in touch with you." Joe Molloy is George Steinbrenner's son-in-law and the Yankees' general partner. Gene Michael was the general manager of the Yankees, who I had heard was stepping down. I told Ed, "It's probably about the general manager's job." My instincts were right. I flew to Tampa to meet with them. I decided down there it wasn't the job I was interested in. Ali was almost eight months pregnant, and with a baby on the way, I wasn't looking to work twenty-five hours a day, thirteen months a year, which is what being general manager for Steinbrenner requires.

A few days later, on October 23, I heard the Yankees had hired Bob Watson to be GM. Bob had played for me in Atlanta, when I managed the Braves. He was a very energetic person who had served me unofficially as a hitting coach. He loved to work with other players in the batting cage. Now he was leaving his job as general manager of the Astros to come to New York. While in Houston, he had overcome prostate cancer. With gallows humor I called him up to congratulate him on his new job.

"Have you gotten yourself checked lately by the doctors?" I said. "Did the doctors tell you you had six months to live? Is that why you took this crazy job?"

I wrote a note to George Steinbrenner thanking him for the interview. "Maybe someday down the road we'll work together," I wrote. I licked the envelope shut and put a stamp on it. That night, before I mailed it, one of my very good friends, Arthur Richman, called me. Arthur had worked as the Mets' public relations director and later traveling secretary while I played and managed there. He works with the Yankees as a senior adviser to Steinbrenner.

"Joe, would you be interested in managing the Yankees?" he said.

"Sure I would," I said. I knew that managing did not require the around-the-clock work hours that being general manager for Steinbrenner required. The manager is responsible only for what happens on the field, while the general manager oversees every facet of the organization.

"It looks like Buck Showalter is leaving," Arthur said, referring to the Yankees' manager, whose contract expired October 31. "George asked me to come up with a list of candidates, and I recommended you. He didn't even know that you're a New Yorker. When I told him that, he got excited. Sit tight. George is going to call you."

I put the note in the mail. About a week later George called me at home.

"You're my man," he said. "We're not doing anything yet and the final say will be up to the general manager, but you're my man. You can pick your own coaches, but I'd like Willie Randolph and Tony Cloninger to stay on, and we're considering Mel Stottlemyre as pitching coach. And if anybody asks you, you can't say you talked to me." George didn't want anyone to think he had started looking for another manager until Showalter officially was gone. We talked for about fifteen minutes. George stressed the importance of loyalty to himself and the organization, and I assured him that that was never going to be a problem with me. We didn't talk about a salary or length of contract. We didn't even talk about a timetable for when I would be hired. A couple of days later, on November 1, Watson called me and told me a prepaid ticket was waiting for me at the Cincinnati airport for a trip to

Tampa. George wanted to meet with me that day and introduce me the next day at a press conference in New York as the new manager of the Yankees.

I telephoned Frank from the airplane on my trip to Tampa. Frank didn't want me to manage at all—I think he was even more bitter about the St. Louis situation than I was.

"You don't need this crap anymore," he said.

"But Frank," I said, "it's too good an opportunity to get to the World Series."

Frank heard the excitement in my voice. He, more than anyone, was aware of my dream. He didn't try to talk me out of it.

"I can tell you want to do this," Frank said. "Go ahead and do it. That's all that counts—you have to do what you want to do. And as long as you're going to manage, this is the perfect job for you."

George told me about the contract: two years, $1.05 million. That was nonnegotiable because that was his offer to Showalter. It was a pay cut for me—I'd earned $550,000 with St. Louis—but I understood. He was taking a lot of heat for losing Showalter, so it wouldn't look good for him to give someone else more money. He also gave me a piece of advice for the press conference. "Just be upbeat." He didn't have to worry about that. I was thrilled. Like everyone else, I had heard all the horror stories about working for George. But I didn't care because of one thing: I knew George was willing to spend the money to win a world championship. It wasn't like St. Louis, where sometimes I had felt as if I were in a fight with my fists while the other guy had a gun. I didn't see any downside. I called up my wife, brothers, sisters, and some friends late that night to let everyone know I was the manager of the Yankees.

The press conference the next day, November 2, was more like an indoor grilling. Showalter had been a popular young manager, and the press looked at my record and figured I was a retread. The line of questioning focused on my losing record. The next day one of the writers referred to me as Clueless Joe. None of it bothered me. I didn't feel that I had to qualify myself to anyone. I told them, "Let's wait and see."

Bob and I flew back to Tampa to meet again with George, this time about my coaching staff. I noticed some people in the Yankee front office called him Mr. Steinbrenner. Not me. I called him George or Boss right from the beginning. That's important to me, because that way I'm talking to him on the same level. I had heard all the stories about how intimidating George can be, but I have never felt pressure being around him. Maybe that was because I didn't expect to get a job like this again. It was a bonus for me.

I liked the idea of trying to get Mel Stottlemyre to be the pitching coach. That was fine. I admired the way he had pitched—he was a no-nonsense guy who wasn't afraid to knock a hitter on his ass—and he had won a world championship as pitching coach for the Mets. George and I agreed that Chris Chambliss would be the hitting coach. I added that I wanted Jose Cardenal as my outfield coach. Jose is a class person, and I think it's important to have a Latin coach on your staff. A manager needs someone to help communicate with his Latin players. It's a bad idea to use a player as your translator because if you have to criticize someone, it should not be done with other players in earshot.

"You've got one more coach," George said. I needed a bench coach. I asked Arthur to give me a list of candidates. I drew up my list. Both lists included Don Zimmer. Though I had often chatted with Zim, we weren't real close friends. I liked the fact that he had managed in four places with an aggressive style, had coached in New York for Steinbrenner, and was very loyal. I called up the sixty-five-year-old Zimmer and said, "So, are you enjoying retirement?"

"Just cashed my first Social Security check," he said.

"I've got a question for you," I said. "How would you like to be my bench coach?"

There was silence on the line. Finally I said, "Well, what do you think?"

"Did George ask you to make this call?"

"No, this is my decision."

"I'll have to think about it."

Zimmer hung up and dialed Billy Connors, the Yankees' organizational pitching coach, and asked him if George had put me up to hiring him. Zim knew no manager wants to have a bench coach forced upon him. He would take the job only if he knew I sincerely wanted him next to me. When Billy assured him it was my decision, he called me back and accepted the job. I got to him just in time, because Buddy Bell, the new Tigers' manager, wanted Zimmer too.

Zim turned out to be the perfect bench coach. I talked more in the dugout than I ever had before, and that's because I ran everything past Zim. When one of my moves didn't work out and I was hard on myself, Don would say, "I should have said this to you . . . ," or, "No, you did the right thing. You'll be fine." We had a great rapport and a lot of fun. We acted silly in the dugout sometimes. He would call me a goof, and I would call him a goof back. So we started a Goof Club. I was Goof I, and he was Goof II. We'd joke about oddball moves during the game—"Hey, Goof I, how about having Cecil Fielder steal a base here," he'd say—and break up laughing. The combination of Zim and me worked so well that it made me think back to how Tim McCarver and I used to talk, when we were Cardinals teammates, about being comanagers someday. It was as stimulating and as fun as Timmy and I had envisioned. Zim and I made such a good team that in one of my telephone conversations with Steinbrenner during the season, I said, "George, how about after you fire me, you put Zim and me in the broadcast booth?" George roared with laughter and said, "No way!"

Five weeks after the Yankees hired me, Ali gave

birth to our daughter, Andrea Rae, who is a miracle in herself. Ali and I had tried for years to have a baby. A few years ago she lost a baby during pregnancy. We talked about adoption. And then all of a sudden along came little Andrea. I was thrilled. People would kid me about having a baby at my age. I'd tell them, "Hey, I'm a fifty-five-year-old man. I have to get up in the middle of the night all the time. She's on *my* schedule."

Ali has been unbelievably supportive. When spring training began, she told me, "You're going to win the World Series this year. This is the year." In August she was telling my daughters from my second marriage, Tina, who lives in England, and Lauren, who lives in Italy, to make plans to be in New York for the World Series. "Would you be quiet?" I said. "It's only August." She'd fire back, "You guys are going to do it. You'll be fine."

Ali and I are such a perfect match that Steinbrenner likes to get on me about being henpecked. I tell him, "You know what? You're right. I can't help it." I have no problem pleading guilty to that charge. It's nice to feel that you want to do something for someone. Ali will tell me, "Don't do it because of me." And I'll tell her, "Why not? Who else am I going to do it for?" The truth is, Ali already has done so much for me. She's made me into a better, happier person—and a much less guarded one. About a month after the World Series, something was bothering me, and I said something to her that nearly caused her to faint right on the spot. I turned one of her favorite lines on her: "Ali, we've got to talk." After a few seconds to recover from the shock, she burst out laughing.

Ali knew how important the World Series dream was to me. And in my first meeting of spring training, I made sure my players understood too.

"Men," I said, "every single one of my coaches has been to the World Series. I haven't. I plan to rectify that this year. I'm determined as hell to get there. One thing you can count on is that I won't manage through the media. If there's something you should know, you're going to hear it from me first. I'm going to do everything I can to eliminate tension on this team. I'll put it in simple terms for you: The one thing I'm interested in is the way we perform on the field, and I'm going to make it as tension-free as possible so that we can devote all of our energy to that."

I thought the meeting went well. As I scanned the room while I talked, I saw the eyes of every player. Nobody was flipping through mail or trying on spikes. I had their attention and I thought this group was serious about winning. I knew we had the potential to win the pennant, especially because of pitchers like David Cone, Jimmy Key, Andy Pettitte, Kenny Rogers, Dwight Gooden, and John Wetteland. It was easily the best pitching staff I ever had as a manager.

On our first day of full workouts in Tampa, outfielders Tim Raines and Gerald Williams showed up on the field after the entire team had run a warm-up lap. I told them, "I don't want to take your money, so you owe me a lap. You can run it at the end of stretching exercises." And they did. I wanted them to know everyone would be treated equally.

That was the most difficult spring training I've ever had because I didn't know very much about my players. I had never played or managed in the American League. I relied a lot on my coaches and Mark Newman, the assistant farm director who did an amazingly efficient job of running a crowded camp of about sixty players at our new facility in Tampa. Stottlemyre, for instance, was the one who convinced me to be confident about Dwight Gooden, even though he was hit hard in spring training. "He's got good pop on the ball," Mel told me. The New York writers were convinced that I believed in Gooden because he was Steinbrenner's personal project. One of them wrote that I rigged an intrasquad game to have Gooden pitch against our reserve and minor league players, instead of our starters, just to make him look good. Not only was that a lie, it was absurd to suggest I would do such a thing.

My six years in the broadcast booth gave me a better understanding of the media and made me more patient with them. But that day forced me to make a decision: either I could stop reading the New York papers and just be as clear and concise as possible with reporters, or I could read the papers and continue to get agitated and overreact enough to distract me from my job. The answer was easy: I would live in a vacuum and not pay any attention to the stuff in the papers, because it doesn't mean anything.

I had more serious problems in spring training anyway. Tim Raines, Tony Fernandez, whom I expected to be my starting second baseman, Pat Kelly, Melido Perez, and Scott Kamieniecki all were hurt in spring training. David Cone concerned me more than Gooden—he had no snap on the ball. And Mariano Rivera, who I had heard had a live arm, showed me an average fastball that was very straight. I knew other teams wanted Rivera, and I told the front office to listen to any deals for him. I don't think they paid attention to me on that suggestion. Rivera started the year as the long man in my bullpen. Jeff Nelson was my setup guy in front of John Wetteland.

I learned very quickly about the mental toughness of my team. After an April Fool's Day opener was snowed out in Cleveland, we beat the defending league champion Indians twice in their own park. By the end of the season and postseason, we would be 18–0 on the road against the Indians, Orioles, and Braves, three of the best teams in baseball.

We didn't fare nearly as well on my nostalgic returns to Milwaukee County Stadium, scene of Frank's magical 1957 World Series home run and my major league debut. The Brewers battered us there in April and in another series in July—including a typical 16–4 rout on my birthday. We were 1–5 in Milwaukee while being outscored 42–22. The way the Brewers smacked us around reminded me of how we used to steal the opposing catcher's signs when I played at County Stadium with the Braves. Our relief pitchers could see the signs from a hut in the outfield bullpen. Only one of them would keep a hat on during a game—he would be the one to relay the signs to the hitter. The pitcher would look straight ahead for a fastball, to the right for a curveball, to the left for a slider, and would put his hand on his head for a change-up.

I don't know for sure if teams still steal signs that way, but the Brewers hit us like they knew what was coming. When teams play you much better in their park than in yours—the Brewers and the Texas Rangers come to mind—it makes you think maybe something is going on. There are a few players who don't like to know what pitch is coming. I found that out when I was catching Lew Burdette with the Braves. He had so much trouble getting Orlando Cepeda out that he resorted to telling him what pitch was coming. He'd say, "Here comes a fastball," and all of a sudden Cepeda couldn't touch him. When he threw his infamous "mystery pitch," he would just mouth the words "wet one." Cepeda was so thrown by Burdette's ploy that he once stepped out of the batter's box and said to the umpire, "Make him stop doing that!" The umpire just shook his head and said, "Nothing I can do."

I don't know how we survived that first month of the season. Jimmy Key, who was coming off major rotator cuff surgery, had no command of his pitches. Cone couldn't spot the ball either because of occasional numbness in his fingers. Gooden was being pelted. Bob Wickman, whom I counted on for important innings out of the bullpen, was a disappointment. The one bright spot was Rivera, whose fastball came alive. As late as April 19 he still was so buried in my bullpen that he pitched three innings of mop-up work in a 7–1 loss in Minnesota. But he threw so well that I decided to try him as a setup man. Three days later he and Wetteland combined for four shutout innings in a 6–2 win over the Royals. All of a sudden my job was a hell of a lot easier. The Formula was born. With Rivera for two innings and Wetteland for one, I knew we could shut down teams after the sixth inning.

During our game the next night, a 5–2 loss to Kansas City, a flyball fell between Bernie Williams and Paul O'Neill in the outfield. I thought O'Neill should have caught the ball, and I told him so. After I removed O'Neill late in the next game, Michael Kay, one of our radio and TV broadcasters, asked me if I was punishing O'Neill. I answered the question, but I didn't like his accusatory manner. When I saw Kay the following night in the middle of our clubhouse, I jumped on his ass.

"Don't fuck with me," I told him. "I don't appreciate you trying to stir up something in the clubhouse. We've got a pretty good chemistry going, and I don't need you to create things to mess it up." I was really angry. If I had seen Kay in a hallway or my office, I would have done it in those places. I happened to see him in the clubhouse. But I admit I didn't mind the players hearing me. It was good for them to know that I do get pissed sometimes.

While I was working out in our exercise room that night, O'Neill came up to me and said, "I read in the papers I'm miffed at you." I said, "I don't read the papers, so you'll have to tell me what they said. Besides, are you miffed?" And he said, "No." So I said, "So it doesn't really matter." I'm proud that I was able to accomplish one of my major goals with the Yankees: to remove the tension in the clubhouse that often is created in New York. Pressure is part of the game, but you shouldn't have tension.

It was shortly after that, on that bus ride to Baltimore April 29, that I called George just to screw around with him. We were 12–10 and tied with the Orioles for first place. "Let's see if we can open up a lead on Baltimore," George said. With my starting pitching problems, I was thinking, let's not get too far behind Baltimore. It turned out to be a landmark series for us. That's where we established our identity as a gritty, determined club with a lot of heart—the mentally toughest team I've ever been around. We fell behind in the first game, 9–4, but came back to win 13–10 in the longest nine-inning game in major league history (four hours, twenty-one minutes). We beat the Orioles again the next night in fifteen innings, 11–6.

Andy Pettitte, who had been knocked out of the previous game in the second inning, showed me a lot of character as he pitched three scoreless innings of relief for the victory. Andy demands so much out of himself that my only concern about him going into the season was that he would get off to a slow start and then make it worse by pressing. Fortunately, we scored a lot of runs for him early when he wasn't pitching well and then he went on a roll. He had a Cy Young award kind of season, but so did Pat Hentgen of the Toronto Blue Jays. When I called Andy after he finished second to Hentgen in the balloting, I heard real disappointment in his voice. He spoke glowingly of Hentgen, but admitted he'd wanted to win it. A lot of guys will tell you, "Oh, it doesn't matter." But I liked hearing Andy say he was disappointed. He is an earnest, hardworking kid who sets high standards for himself.

After our two-game sweep in Baltimore, David Cone kept us on the winning track when he pitched a brilliant five-hitter to beat Chicago 5–1. But his circulatory problem would not go away. When doctors discovered an aneurysm two days after that start, I figured he was gone for the season. Fortunately, just as Cone went down, the old Doc Gooden came back. On May 8, the day we put Coney on the disabled list, Gooden won his first game in almost two years, having spent almost all of that time on baseball's suspended list for drug use.

On May 14, Gooden's next start, Bill Cosby called our public relations department asking for tickets to that game against Seattle. I met Bill through Bob Gibson while I was playing for the Cardinals. Bill has become a good friend who is such a kind person that he once did seventy-five minutes of comedy at a charity dinner Ali and I helped organize in St. Louis, then refused to accept a fee. Bill planned to stop by the clubhouse before the game to visit the players. He canceled at the last minute. Cos missed a hell of a game. Gooden had a no-hitter and a 2–0 lead with runners at second and third in the ninth inning and one out. He struck out Jay Buhner. The next batter was a left-handed hitter, Paul Sorrento, with a right-hander, Dan Wilson, on deck.

"Who's the next hitter?" Zimmer asked me. I've learned that when Zim says that, it's his key to suggest a strategic move.

"Wilson," I said.

"Want to put this guy on?" Zimmer said to me.

"Don't bother messing around with me now," I told him. "He's walked six guys already. I can't do that. I may be sorry later if this guy whacks one, but I can't do that. The last thing I want to do is load the bases where he has to throw a strike."

We got lucky. Gooden threw Sorrento a high breaking ball but got away with it. Sorrento popped it up. Dwight had his no-hitter. I never was fortunate enough to catch a no-hitter, though I did play third base when Bob Gibson no-hit the Pittsburgh Pirates in 1971. I'm not superstitious enough to avoid saying "no-hitter" when a guy is throwing one—that's supposed to be the ultimate jinx—though as Dwight rolled on I didn't move from my seat after the fifth inning, even though I felt a pressing need to go to the bathroom. The most amazing part of the night was that he no-hit probably the greatest offensive machine I've ever seen. The Mariners could beat you by belting home runs and manufacturing runs. It was tremendous to watch Dwight leave the field on his teammates' shoulders, pumping his arms and screaming with joy. It seemed like he had been walking on egg-shells after his suspension from the game for drug abuse, and a lot of emotions came pouring out. The victory kept us two and a half games ahead of Balti-more, with a 22–14 record. Dwight really gave us a lift while Cone was out. He pitched well until his arm grew weary late in the season. He wasn't equipped to pitch a lot of innings after being out of baseball that long. And when Gooden did falter, Cone came back just in time to replace him.

We hit our first stretch of poor play on a West Coast trip in May, losing four of the first six games. Some guys were getting careless in their work hab-its. Base runners and batters were missing signs. When we opened a series in Oakland May 31, I decided we needed what I call a red ass meeting.

I'm not a screamer and I don't throw things in the clubhouse, but I do have a temper. I get real worked up when I'm angry. I'm very forceful with my words. And I made sure I let my team know I was angry.

"This is the best chance I've ever had to get to the World Series," I told them. "I'm determined to work hard to do it. And if it takes making your life miserable, that's what I'm going to do. If I didn't think we had the team to do it, then it wouldn't bother me. But I sure as hell know we do have the team to do it. And when you're not doing all the things you need to do to win, that's when this shit has to stop. I'm an easy manager to play for. But when you're making mistakes that you shouldn't make—and it has nothing to do with striking out or making errors—then I can make your life miserable."

I remember in that meeting I singled out a few players, such as Ruben Sierra and Bernie Williams, for making too many mental mistakes. After the meeting was over I walked around the clubhouse, kind of taking inventory. I could tell something wasn't right with Bernie.

"You all right?" I said. "What's the matter?"

"You didn't get on Boggs," he said.

Bernie's a smart guy who doesn't miss too much. He knew that during a recent game Wade Boggs had made a mistake on the bases by not knowing how many outs there were at the time. I pulled out my notes for the meeting and showed Bernie I had written down Wade Boggs's name, too, but had forgotten to get on him.

"I thought you didn't get on him just because he's a future Hall of Famer," Bernie said.

"No, I just forgot," I told him.

I made sure that I got on Boggs in the dugout in front of everybody. I did it in a different kind of way—more lighthearted than my mood in the meeting—about not keeping track of the number of outs. I wanted everyone, including Bernie, to know that in my quest to get to the World Series, everybody would be treated equally.

It was during that series that Sierra called me a liar, claiming I had reneged on a promise to play him in the outfield instead of as the designated hitter. I didn't worry about it too much. I just considered the source. Ruben was the toughest guy I ever had to manage. As much as I tried to talk to him about the team concept of baseball, he just never did get it. I guess a long time ago somebody must have decided, "He has a great deal of ability. Just leave him alone," because Ruben has no clue what baseball is about. That was evident when he came back to New York after we traded him to Detroit. He thought he was ripping the Yankees when he said, "All they care about over there is winning." That told you everything you needed to know about Ruben Sierra. He announced to the world that he cared only about his statistics, regardless of whether his team won or not. The day after Ruben said that, Tigers' manager Buddy Bell came up to me and said, "He's going to find out we want to win too." Ruben doesn't play for Detroit anymore. He's now with Cincinnati, his fifth team in six years.

It took time for me to understand what Sierra was all about. We made him our project in spring training. He came in heavy, and we worked to get some weight off him. We had Chris Chambliss work with him on his hitting, José Cardenal on his outfield play, and Reggie Jackson on all aspects of his game, including his mental approach. He did okay in the outfield. His feet got quicker as we worked with him. But Ruben is like a spoiled kid. He wants everything his way. He always thought he should have been playing right field instead of Paul O'Neill. He always thought he should be wearing number 21, his old number, instead of O'Neill.

When Tim Raines started the season on the disabled list, I told Ruben, "You can't play the outfield. Gerald Williams is playing left field. I can't put you in left field and DH Gerald Williams. He is a better defensive player. I can't do that." But Ruben would never acknowledge that he understood what I was talking about or that it was the right thing to do. I'd talk to him, I'd put my arms around him, I'd be positive around him—it was a lot of work. And he still didn't get it.

Every time he didn't play, he was moping. I'd explain to him why he wouldn't be playing against a certain pitcher, and he never understood. When he called me a liar, I told him, "Look, when I say something, I mean it. But when things change, like Raines getting hurt, my thoughts change."

Finally I went to Bob Watson and told him, "Get rid of Sierra." Somehow, some way, Bob made a deal for Cecil Fielder on July 31, in which he convinced the Tigers to take Sierra. He should have been named executive of the year right on the spot.

The only other guy who really gave me some grief was Jimmy Leyritz, and that was only because Jimmy's a proud guy who objected to me pulling him for a pinch hitter. I took him out in a situation where I wanted a left-handed batter facing a right-handed pitcher. I didn't think it was such a big deal. After all, I wasn't afraid to hit for former batting champions like Wade Boggs and Paul O'Neill to get what I thought to be better matchups. But Jimmy made a scene in the dugout about it. I felt he was showing me up. The next day I met privately with him and told him I didn't appreciate the way he acted. Jimmy told me, "I'm a better hitter the bigger the situation. I rise to the occasion"—words I would recall distinctly when he hit a huge home run in Game Four of the World Series. I told Jimmy, "I'm glad you're a better hitter in big situations. But if I'm going to pinch-hit for you or anybody, I'm going to pinch-hit. I'm going to do what I can to win the game."

We played better after I chewed out the team in Oakland, winning all three games there. But I had something else to worry about: My brother Frank was sick at his home in Florida, and the doctors could not pinpoint what was wrong. I talked with him every day, and he sounded worse with each conversation. Frank's friends would call me up—as many as six of them a day—and say, "Have you talked to Frank lately? He doesn't sound good. You've got to do something." Those guys were driving me nuts.

Frank said his stomach hurt, and he felt so lethargic that he didn't even feel like getting out of bed and walking across the room. Doctors removed his gallbladder, which they called the worst-diseased gallbladder they had ever seen. Frank felt a little better after having it removed, but he quickly deteriorated again. The doctors couldn't pinpoint the problem. I noticed something terrible in his voice. The world's greatest needler, the guy who would battle you with all his might at everything from cards to golf, and the guy who toughened me up, wanted to quit. He was ready to die. Now it was my turn to return the favor. I pushed Frank to keep fighting. My first order of business was to get him into a better hospital in New York. He refused, saying he didn't feel up to the trip.

While I was worried about Frank, George called me and Stottlemyre up to his office on June 18. George called Watson frequently during the season to complain about players if they weren't producing. He's very reactionary. Every once in a while he would suggest I bench someone, take a pitcher out of the rotation, or send someone to the minors.

Never did I make any decision like that because he suggested it. Anytime I did make a personnel decision, it was for one reason: I thought it was best for the team.

He also loved to blame my coaching staff when things went wrong, which I can understand because it's part of his football mindset. If a guy wasn't hitting, it was the fault of Chris Chambliss, my hitting coach. If the bullpen was struggling, it was the fault of Tony Cloninger, my bullpen coach. One my outfielders, Gerald Williams, had a bad habit of trying to pick up a rolling ball with his bare hand. Every once in a while he would drop the ball, and whenever he did, George would complain to me that Jose Cardenal, my outfield coach, wasn't doing his job. But I knew Cardenal worked with Gerald constantly to get him to field the ball with his glove. My coaching staff worked long and hard, so they shouldn't be blamed for players' mistakes.

George would second-guess me sometimes about game decisions too. That didn't bother me. I was harder on myself than anyone else when things didn't work out. But George never second-guessed me on the same decisions on which I beat myself up. He never hit on the same nerve, so his second-guessing never rattled me.

Steinbrenner wasn't second-guessing when he called Mel and me up to his office that day in June. He was worried about a day-night doubleheader we were scheduled to play in Cleveland in two days. I planned to pitch two rookies against the Indians,

Brian Boehringer and Ramiro Mendoza. George was afraid we were going to get embarrassed by a powerful Indians team in his hometown.

"We can't go into Cleveland with these two kids," he told us. "What else can we do? Can we call up somebody from the minors with more experience? What about Wally Whitehurst?"

Maybe it's because everything else seemed small compared with Frank's problems, but I told George, "Don't worry about it, Boss. We'll win. And if we lose, it's not going to be because of our starting pitchers. Besides, Mel already told Mendoza he's starting. Do you want to circumvent my pitching coach's authority and just negate his credibility?"

Eventually George said, "Fine, but it's your ass that's on the line."

We fell behind Cleveland in the opener of that Friday doubleheader 5–1, then staged one of our patented rallies to win in ten innings 8–7. One of the most important elements in our ability to come from behind was our bullpen. I knew we had enough good arms there to hold the team down to enable us to come back. I also hammered home the importance of thinking small, of chipping away at deficits rather than trying to make them up in one giant chunk—a philosophy that would never be more important than in Game Four of the World Series. I like my team to play the first six innings of a game as if the score is 0–0. Even if we're down by four or five runs, for instance, I'll continue to steal bases up until the seventh or eighth inning, when the urgency of the situation forces you to be more conservative. We did a terrific job of doing whatever we could to get one run at a time, no matter how much we trailed.

It was a huge win, coming back like that on the road against a team like Cleveland. I walked back to the visiting manager's office at Jacobs Field feeling great. We had about two hours to kill before the second game, so we ate dinner in the clubhouse. And then about thirty minutes before the second game, the telephone rang. It was Ali.

"Are you sitting down?" she said. I immediately thought that Frank, who was in a hospital in Florida, had died.

"Rocco died," she said.

I was in shock. I couldn't believe it. Ali started crying.

"What are you going to do?" she said between sobs.

"Let me think for a minute," I said. "I'll call you back." I told Arthur Richman, who was in the room with me, what had happened. He started crying. Then I called Rocco's wife, Rose. She told me Rocco had been watching our game on television. We were losing in the ninth inning, and Rocco said, "They haven't won one of these games all year." Rose said, "There's always a first time." And we did come back to win. Then Rose said to him, "What would you like for dinner? Would you like to go out, or do you want to cook something here?"

Rocco didn't answer. He just reached up and grabbed both sides of his head and fell over. He was dead from a heart attack.

I called Ali back. I said, "He's gone. There's nothing I can do. My responsibility is here. I'll come home Sunday."

Word spread through the clubhouse about Rocco. John Wetteland walked into my office and expressed his sympathy.

"What's your sister-in-law's name?" he asked.

"Rose," I said. "Why?"

"I want to pray for her," he said.

I went right back to work. We won the second game 9–3, behind Mendoza. We won again on Saturday 11–9, with another big comeback after being down 5–0 to Dennis Martinez. Then on Sunday, in a game we would win 6–5, I left in the second inning to fly home. I said good-bye to Rocco that night, and we buried him the next morning. Before the casket was closed, I placed in it my lineup card from the first game of the Friday doubleheader, the last game Rocco ever saw. I also put my cap in the casket and a baseball autographed by all my players.

Rocco was sixty-eight when he died. My father was sixty-eight when he died. My mother was sixty-nine when she died. Frank was two months away from his sixty-fifth birthday when he received his new heart. I am very aware of my own mortality and the prevalence of heart disease in my family history. I undergo an extensive, high-tech stress test at least every two years, including as recently as

January 1997. My friend and cardiologist, Dr. Joe Platania, tells me my heart is functioning normally. With my beloved Rocco gone, I wonder if his fancy machines can tell that it is also a little bit broken.

About a week before the all-star game, Indians' manager Mike Hargrove called me to say he wanted me to be one of his all-star coaches. I gratefully accepted. Three days later I called him back and said, "Mike, I hope you don't mind if I back out. I have a new baby and I haven't been able to spend a lot of time at home. Plus, I'm exhausted." Mike said he understood and wished me luck. He had sent me a very nice note after Rocco died, and later, after we won the World Series, he sent me another sensitive letter congratulating me.

At the same time, George signed Darryl Strawberry from the independent Northern League. He sent him to Triple-A Columbus to get some at bats. I was reluctant to have Darryl. I hadn't heard too much that was good about the guy, especially concerning his past problems with alcohol, drugs, women, and the IRS. When reporters asked me if signing Darryl was my idea, I told them, "It's an organizational decision." George was ready to bring him up right away to the Yankees. He kept asking me, "Do you want him for this game?" And I'd say, "No, let's just wait." Finally I decided to bring up Darryl on the day before the all-star break. I knew his arrival would create a genuine New York circus, and I didn't want that to distract us from a big four-game series right after the break in Baltimore.

I preferred to sacrifice our last home game before the break (and we did lose, 4–1) than mess with that Baltimore series.

Darryl told me on his first day in New York, "I'll do whatever you want me to do."

"I only judge people from the day I meet them," I said, "and see how they play for me. I only deal with effort. I know you can't always perform like you want to, but you can always try."

I never had a bit of a problem with Darryl. He played very well for us and, by stealing some bases and playing hard, gave us some energy in addition to some big home runs.

George called me at my office in Baltimore before we opened the series against the Orioles. We had a six-game lead. "You have to split these four games," he said.

"It depends what happens early," I said. "If we win the first game, a split may not be enough. If we win the first two, a split will definitely not be enough. And if we win the first three, we'll want a sweep. We'll be fine, George."

We won the first game 4–2, with a rally in the eighth inning. We won the second game 3–2, with a rally in the ninth inning. And after we won the third game 7–5, I knew we would win the fourth. The Orioles were a dead club at that point. You can't lose so many close games at home without being demoralized. We finished the sweep behind Pettitte, 4–1, to take a ten-game lead. By July 28 our lead was up to twelve games. I felt good, but I knew the race wasn't over, not after the whole world watched the California Angels blow a big lead the previous season.

Meanwhile I kept badgering Frank to come to New York for better medical help. A friend of ours, Sy Berger, had recommended Columbia-Presbyterian Medical Center in Manhattan. I told Frank about it, and he seemed ready to make the trip, but then he said, "I can't stand to go through any more tests. I'm worn out." But the next day, Saturday, August 3, he finally gave in.

"I made up my mind," he said. "I'm coming up Tuesday."

"Great. I'll be there to pick you up," I said.

I hadn't seen Frank since spring training. He hadn't been feeling great then, but he was walking around and looked fine. Frank is a tall man—six foot four—and has always had a strong constitution. When he came off the plane, being pushed in a wheelchair, I hardly recognized him. He was a frail, crooked old man, a shadow of his former self. As we waited at the baggage claim, I couldn't believe this was my brother. He sat slumped in the chair, rubbing his eyes and not having enough strength to lift his head. I was afraid that my big brother, one of the toughest men I've ever known, was dying.

Before entering Columbia-Presbyterian, Frank removed his 1957 World Series ring and handed it to his wife. He didn't want to lose it there while undergoing tests. It was the first time he had taken it off his finger since he earned it thirty-nine years ago. The people at the hospital did a fantastic job. They stabilized Frank within two days with a drug that could only be administered intravenously. He felt comfortable, but his heart was giving out. Until a new one was located—the right match at the right time when his name moved to the top of the donor recipient list—Frank had to be tethered to a machine. There was nothing he could do but wait.

As Frank felt better, George felt worse. When our lead shrank to eight games in mid-August, I could hear the first signs of panic in George's voice. He called me up one day at my office at Yankee Stadium with a warning. "Joe," he said, "if you blow this thing, they'll never let you forget it. You'll have to live with it the rest of your life. You'll be another Ralph Branca." I immediately thought back to Bobby Thomson's home run and the Dodgers' thirteen-game lead in mid-August. I just wanted to get it out of my mind.

I didn't dwell on it, but we still hit a slump. We lost one game in Chicago in which Jeter tried to steal third base in the eighth inning of a tie game with Fielder batting. He was thrown out. I was pissed, especially at myself. Even though Jeter had run on his own, I should have given him the sign *not* to run in that situation. I made the mistake of assuming that a rookie would know to let Cecil swing the bat in that situation. I was so mad that I didn't want to go over and talk to him, for fear I'd start screaming at him. I said to myself, He's still a kid; calm down. So what did Jeter do? He came over and sat next to me in the dugout so I could yell at him and get it over with.

Jeter constantly impressed me with his poise. I liked him even before I met him. Before spring training I told reporters that he was going to be my shortstop. They were surprised, especially because we also had Tony Fernandez, an established shortstop. When asked about it, Jeter said, "I'm going to get an *opportunity* to play shortstop." I liked his answer better than mine. During a winter conference call with George and his advisers, Gene Michael, one of our scouts, said to me, "You're going to have to be patient with Jeter. He's made some errors in the past, but he'll get better. He may not be ready from day one." Then George said, "I better not come up to Yankee Stadium until July. I might not like what I see."

I was concerned about Jeter myself, only because when you rely on pitching you have to have a shortstop who can catch the ball. He worked very hard in spring training and I thought he would be okay. Late in spring training, though, George walked into my office and said, "My advisers tell me they don't think Jeter is ready to play." I said, "Well, it's too late for that now, folks." We had already made our commitment. And once the season started, it was as if he jumped into a phone booth and changed into a Superman costume. I received two pleasant surprises on opening day: a huge good-luck basket of goodies from my friend Big

Julie Isaacson and a stunning performance by Jeter. The rookie made a great catch of a pop fly and hit a home run—signs of things to come. He played steady shortstop all year and stayed away from long slumps at the plate. There is one other thing about Jeter that I like: He always calls me Mr. Torre.

Like Jeter, Wetteland gave us invaluable consistency. But on August 16 we had to put him on the disabled list with a pulled groin muscle. Our starting pitchers tried to cover his loss by pitching better and longer, a dangerous mindset that often resulted in them getting tattooed in the first inning. By the time we left for a West Coast trip August 25, our lead was down to six games over Baltimore. The Mariners swept us three straight in Seattle, cutting it to four games. We had lost eight games off our lead in twenty-nine days. In the finale of that series Seattle kicked the crap out of us 10–2 and rubbed in the pain by throwing a pitch at Paul O'Neill. Paulie thought Mariners' manager Lou Piniella, his former manager in Cincinnati, had ordered the hit, and Paul started a bench-clearing fight when he challenged the Seattle dugout. O'Neill and Jeter were like knockdown dolls at a county fair all year; pitchers threw at them with regularity. Our pitchers didn't do a good enough job defending our own people. You can't let those knockdowns go unanswered, or else you're allowing yourself to be intimidated.

In this case Jeff Nelson did hit somebody, though I wish he had gone after somebody bigger.

He hit a jockey: Joey Cora, their little second base-man. Our situation was getting urgent. For the first and only time all season, I held a meeting immediately after the game, trying to light a fire under my team.

First I told my pitchers they had to do a better job of defending our hitters. "Don't let anybody ever think they can intimidate us," I said. And then I challenged my players.

"Now we'll see what we're made of, boys," I said. "This is a man's game. People are coming after you. Now let's see how you respond."

I guess my speech didn't exactly fire up the troops: We got clobbered the next night in California, 14–3. After that loss, with a six o'clock start scheduled for the next night, I announced in the clubhouse, "I don't want to see anybody in here until an hour before the game tomorrow. Don't even bother showing up before then. No batting practice, no nothing."

I sensed that the players were trying too hard. Pettitte made me look good by pitching eight strong innings that next game in a 6–2 win, running his record after losses to 12–2. The next time I want to have a meeting, I'll make sure I do it when Pettitte is my starting pitcher.

I felt so relieved about getting that win that I played golf the next day at Newport Country Club with Reggie Jackson, Gene Mauch (who played and managed in 4,245 games without getting to the World Series), and Zimmer. That was some foursome: Mr. October, Mr. Never Been to October, Mr. Wishing All His Life for October—and the little round guy we call Popeye. I'm not very good at golf, but it's a good getaway when you need a break from baseball. The season is such a long grind that I think it's necessary to occasionally make time for something else. I know that doesn't fit perfectly with George's thinking. He doesn't allow anyone on the club to travel with golf bags, which is fine— that discourages people from playing too much. But I and some coaches would pack golf shoes and balls and play once or twice on the longer trips. On the first West Coast trip Zim and I got up at five o'clock in the morning to play in Los Angeles. I found playing with rented clubs actually helped my game—I upgraded from terrible to bad.

On that same trip to Anaheim I decided we needed Bernie Williams to raise the level of his game. Bernie has tremendous skills, but he's such a quiet person that he was difficult for me to read sometimes. In fact, I called Don Mattingly, the former Yankee first baseman, once during the season just to talk about Bernie. Don had played with Bernie for several years and knew him much better than I did. He told me he noticed that Bernie played great toward the end of 1995, when he was moved from sixth to second in the batting order. Based on that conversation, I thought I had to keep Bernie high in the batting order—second or third, mostly—to get the most out of him.

In Anaheim I noticed that Bernie was stuck in

one of these phases I would see from time to time
where he doesn't play aggressively in the outfield.
It's not that he wasn't hustling. He just wasn't getting good jumps on the ball. He wasn't making the
plays he should make. I walked up to him in center
field during batting practice and told him, "Bernie,
I want you to know how important you are to this
ball club. This team looks to you for leadership. I
don't mean being vocal in the clubhouse. It's just
the way you carry yourself. The rest of the team
responds to your presence, just because of all the
great things you can do on the field. That's the kind
of player you are."

Bernie looked at me with those big, soft eyes of
his like I had just told him a secret. He was
shocked. He thought he was just another one of the
guys on the team.

"I'd pay my own money to watch you play, that's
the kind of special talent you have," I said.

He liked the sound of that. He smiled. Everyone
else on the club was smiling, too, when David Cone
returned to pitch September 2. We had a four-game
lead, with twenty-six games to play. Coney gave us
a big psychological lift by being back with us. No
one expected he would throw seven no-hit innings
in his first game in three months. I wasn't even
close to letting him finish the game. I would have
been jeopardizing his career, because he didn't have
the arm strength yet to throw a complete game. I
had had to do the same thing with a pitcher named
Tommy Boggs when I was managing the Braves.

He had a no-hitter going in his first start after reha-
bilitating his arm, but I had to take him out.

Cone is the kind of competitor who always wants
the ball. After the seventh inning he told me, "If
you leave it up to me, I'll stay in there. I understand it's your call." I told him, "I'm not going to
risk losing you. Nice job." I later received a letter
from somebody telling me I owed it to the fans to
allow Cone to try for the no-hitter. That's too ro-
mantic. I have to be concerned about his health
more than about fairy tales. My man Bernie, with
his newly pumped-up ego, preserved the no-hitter
with a great catch at the wall in center field. Mariano Rivera lost the no-hitter on an infield hit in the
ninth inning, but we were thrilled to know that we
had Cone back.

Surprisingly, the lift Cone gave us didn't last.
We became tentative. The Orioles seemed like they
were winning every day, and we could hear their
footsteps. On September 9, a travel day for us to
Detroit, our lead was down to two and a half
games, with twenty games to go. I didn't like the
look of my team at that time. When guys walked
into the clubhouse for work, they weren't holding
their heads up high. We were timid. I decided I
would have a meeting the next day.

Tiger Stadium has one of the smallest visiting
clubhouses in baseball. With its narrow, chicken-
wire lockers and pillars in the middle of the room,
it probably hasn't changed much since Joe DiMaggio played there. I didn't mind that. It just meant

my team would be huddled closer together when I addressed them.

"The only people we have are each other," I told them. "Everybody is looking to place blame, and if you want to do that, go ahead. It's there for you. Just be warned that you're going to be inundated with people trying to find out reasons why you're not winning and why your lead is cut. If you start pointing fingers, things are going to break down and get ugly.

"One thing I want you to remember: We're a better team than Baltimore. We've beaten them, and we're going to beat them. And do you know why? We have more heart than they do. We don't have any selfish players here. We're going to get this thing done. Believe me, we're going to win this."

As the players scattered to get ready to play, Zimmer said to me, "You lied."

"What are you talking about?" I said.

"You said we didn't have any selfish players here," he said.

"I know. Just leave this thing to me, will ya?" I said.

I knew what Zim was talking about. We did have a couple of players who may have been overly concerned sometimes about their own numbers. But you really don't have to tell your team that. The players know who among them has a selfish streak. Anyway, I believed my club was a lot tougher mentally than Baltimore. I remember back in April, when Davey Johnson took Cal Ripken out of a close game because he wanted a faster runner. I never thought anything about it; a manager tries to win every game he can. But I detected that a hush came over the crowd. And Cal just sat there on the bench through extra innings and didn't move, obviously upset about coming out.

I detected more individualism on their team than ours, probably because they had so many all-star players with strong personalities, beginning right from spring training, when Bobby Bonilla complained about being a DH. Later on they stopped the game and had a big ceremony when Eddie Murray hit his five hundredth home run. That's a great accomplishment, but anytime you stop the game and put the focus on an individual, that's distracting. It takes away from the flow of the game and contributes to the idea of an individual playing the game for his own rewards instead of for the purpose of winning. Knowing Eddie, he was probably more uncomfortable than anybody about the fanfare. As I told my ball club, I knew we had more heart than Baltimore. It's the one intangible that makes the difference between a first-place team and the rest of the pack.

We won that day of my speech—barely. Ruben Rivera saved a 9–8 victory with a diving catch in right field. I shudder to think what might have happened if the kid hadn't caught that ball. That win started us on a six-one trip, bringing us home to a showdown series with the Orioles. We had a three-game lead, with twelve games to play. We had to win at least one of the three games with Baltimore to hold them off. After a rainout we were two outs away from losing the opener when Bernie tied the game with a single. We won it 3–2, in the tenth inning, on a single by Ruben Rivera.

The next day, a doubleheader, I pitched Kenny Rogers in the first game against Mike Mussina and David Cone in the second game. I explained to Cone that I didn't want Kenny waiting around for the second game; I was afraid he would get too jumpy. Cone has the perfect attitude about those kinds of things. He's a confident professional who'll do whatever you ask. Kenny outpitched Mussina in the first game, a 9–3 win. I knew then the race was over. Even though we lost the second game of the doubleheader, we had a four-game lead with ten games to play. I knew we weren't going to blow that.

The official clincher happened on September 25, in the first game of a doubleheader at home against Milwaukee. We pounded the Brewers 19–2. I was thrilled that Ali, Andrea, and my sisters were at the game to share the moment with me. Streamers and confetti fell like snow from the upper deck. The standings and the Orioles didn't matter anymore. We were East Division champions.

The only decision I had to make in that clinching game was about who to pitch the ninth inning. I wanted somebody who had been with us all year. I thought it was the perfect spot for Jeff Nelson. Nellie is a six-foot-eight right-hander with nasty stuff, but he had been inconsistent. His ego could use the boost of being in the middle of the clinching celebration. It worked. Nellie came up to me a couple of days later and thanked me for the opportunity to get the clinching out. That's why it's important for a manager to know his players. You try to figure out what they need and put them in a position where they can succeed. That's one of Jimmy Leyland's favorite lines. I knew a small decision like that could pay dividends in the postseason.

After the clincher Wade Boggs and Tino Martinez asked me if they could have a beer. They weren't playing in the second game, so I said, "Sure, go ahead and celebrate." The rest of us made do with bottled water, saving the champagne for later. I felt elation and relief at the same time. The season had been grueling, especially because of the anxiety of the lead shrinking from twelve games to two and a half. I thought about the pain Frank's 1956 Braves team must have felt when it squandered a lead to the Dodgers, or how the 1951 Dodgers couldn't hold off the charge of the Giants—the race going down to the last swing of the bat. I was glad to avoid that kind of infamy.

While I was hugging my players, someone told me there was a telephone call for me in my office. I knew it was Steinbrenner, calling to congratulate me. I picked up the phone with a big grin on my face.

"Hello," I said, "this is Bobby Thomson."

CHAPTER 8
October, at Last

I WAS ELATED TO WIN THE EAST DIVI-
sion, but I felt relief more than anything after
spending the second half of the season clinging
to our lead. That long grind and the anxiety of
watching our lead get sliced from twelve games to
two and a half didn't matter anymore. Now, in the
playoffs, everyone was even again. It would be a
matter of which team hit a hot streak. Of the three
rounds of playoffs, I felt the most pressure before
our Division Series against the Texas Rangers, because if we lost that series, very few people would
remember the 1996 Yankees. The Yankees franchise
has a tradition of excellence and high expectations.
Everything we accomplished during the regular
season would be diminished if we were bounced in
the first round by a team that was making its first
trip ever to the postseason.

I had two major decisions to make for the series: Do I pitch Jimmy Key or Kenny Rogers in Game Three? And do I start Darryl Strawberry or Cecil Fielder as my designated hitter in Game One? Key had been hit hard in his last start, and Rogers had pitched well in each of his past two starts. I decided on Key as my pitcher and told him and Rogers in the outfield during a workout on the next to last day of the season. I trusted Jimmy with the pressure of the postseason. He had been there before, and Kenny had not.

Before our workout on the eve of Game One against Texas, Darryl walked into my office and said, "Why don't you play Big Daddy, because I can handle not playing."

"I understand that," I said, "and I appreciate you telling me that. You've let me off the hook. But I'm still going to play you."

Strawberry had had good statistics batting against the Texas starter, John Burkett, when they played in the National League. I understood they were old numbers. But I looked for Strawberry to be pumped. I expected him to rise to the challenge of the postseason. He's not afraid of the competition. I was playing a hunch.

I explained my decision to Cecil and said, "I know you're not happy about it. I'm going to tell the writers that I'll make up my mind tomorrow. And tomorrow no writers are allowed in the clubhouse before the game, so you don't even have to deal with them. And unless Darryl just goes lights out, you'll be in there for Game Two."

I knew he was disappointed. As it turned out, I think it drove Cecil a little more. That wasn't the reason I did it, but I think it helped. Since then Cecil made some comments about being angry about not playing and having a problem with our communication. I pride myself on maintaining dialogue with my players. It took me a long time to make that decision about starting Darryl. I really wrestled with it. And when I did tell Cecil about it, I made sure I explained it and protected him from the media. Communication is very important to me. All year long, whenever I didn't play one of my regulars, I made sure to tell that player myself. I don't like sending one of my coaches to do that kind of work. It makes it easier to sleep. You do your own dirty work. If it turned out that I lit a fire under Cecil, it wasn't by design.

My hunch didn't pan out. Darryl was hitless in four at bats. We struggled against Burkett and lost 6–2. Burkett jammed the hell out of us, giving a perfect example of why it's important to pitch inside, to be able to get people out with pitches away. Too many pitchers today nibble at the outside corner of the plate with breaking balls. They're afraid to come inside, thinking if they don't get the ball inside enough, it can wind up in the outfield seats.

Burkett, by relying on a hard inside fastball, pitched the kind of game that used to be associated with the National League. As recently as about ten years ago, the American League was known as a breaking ball league and the National League as a fastball league. Ted Simmons, my old teammate with the Cardinals, struggled when he was traded to the Milwaukee Brewers in 1981 because every time he thought it was a fastball count, the AL pitchers would throw him a breaking ball. Now both leagues are breaking ball leagues. The biggest difference between the leagues is that the AL has more power, so managers tend to sit around and wait for home runs. Most AL teams don't send the runner with a full count on the batter. So-called running counts don't come into play in the AL like they do in the NL, mostly because of the DH. An AL manager doesn't have to worry about trying to score before the pitcher's spot in the lineup comes up.

My background, as well as Zimmer's aggressive style, gave us the look of an NL team. Some people criticized us in the second half of the season for being less creative after we acquired Strawberry and Fielder. But we fell behind early in a lot of games in the second half, which limits how bold you can be, and other teams began to catch on to us and did a better job anticipating when we would bunt, steal a base, or execute a hit-and-run play.

Steinbrenner walked into my office after Game One looking very distraught. "We've got to win three out of four now," he said.

"We can do that," I said. The truth is, I was scared to death after that first game. We were inept.

I knew in a best-of-five series, we had to turn it around immediately. We had one more game at Yankee Stadium before the series moved to Texas, where we had lost five out of six games during the season. In Game Two, with Pettitte pitching, we fell behind 4–1 after three innings. Texas scored all of its runs on two home runs by Juan Gonzalez, his second and third of the series. Gonzalez was absolutely awesome. He hit pitches out of the ballpark whether we pitched him inside or outside. If I was ever going to walk someone intentionally with nobody on base, he would be the guy. But I didn't like the idea of putting one of my pitchers in a position where he has to throw strikes to the hitter coming up after him. It's a lot more comfortable to pitch when you don't have to throw strikes than when you do.

We chipped away at the Rangers until we tied the game at four in the eighth inning, on a base hit by Fielder. I had two thoughts at the time: We can beat the Rangers bullpen, and we should try to make Texas third baseman Dean Palmer handle the ball as much as we can. I noticed that he was having problems throwing the ball.

Texas put a scare into us in the twelfth inning. Graeme Lloyd started the inning for me, but I replaced him with Nelson after he gave up a base hit. Nelson struck out two batters, but then Gonzalez got a base hit. Then I replaced Nelson with Rogers because Will Clark, a left-handed hitter, was batting. Kenny walked Clark on four pitches. Then I replaced Rogers with Brian Boehringer. My only remaining relief pitcher was David Weathers, who had pitched two innings in Game One. Boehringer retired Palmer on a fly ball. We used four pitchers to get three outs in a half inning that took twenty-four minutes, and I came out looking like a genius. The reality is, I had no other choice but to use Boehringer in that spot. I was lucky. Those situations have a better chance of working out in Johnny Parascandola's basement with APBA cards than they do in the big leagues.

Derek Jeter, who started or finished as many big rallies for us as anyone, opened the bottom of the twelfth inning with a single. Tim Raines walked. Then I asked Charlie Hayes to bunt. He made the right play by bunting it to Palmer. The third baseman fielded the ball cleanly but threw it wildly to first base. The ball may have been slippery because of the light rain that was falling. Jeter came running home with the winning run.

It was almost two o'clock in the morning by the time we boarded the team buses that would take us to the airport for our trip to Texas. One bus was reserved for coaches, my staff, and front office personnel, including some women. I sat down in the first row on the right-hand side on the aisle. George was sitting in the row behind me, on the aisle. And then Reggie Jackson walked in.

"Here, sit next to me, Reggie," I said and scooted over to make room for him. Reggie hadn't been around the ball club often during the regular season. When the playoffs were about to begin, he had asked me if he should come in from his home in California. "Sure, come on in," I said. That was my mistake. I had wanted him there, but Reggie doesn't work for me. He works for George. I should have cleared it with the Boss.

"What are you doing here?" Steinbrenner snapped, sort of half kidding when he saw Reggie on the bus. George seemed miffed for a couple of reasons: He hadn't known Reggie would be traveling with us, and Reggie was sitting in front of him.

"You want me to leave?" Reggie said.

"No," George said, "but next time I want to know about your schedule—where you're going and where you plan to be every day."

I could feel Reggie bubbling like water on a stove. He jumped out of his seat and started going after George. I grabbed him around his shoulders, but Reggie threw me off him like a matchstick. He leaned down toward George, who was sitting down, and got right in his face.

"I'm sick of the way you talk down to me! Don't mess with me anymore!"

"Why don't you relax and sit down," George said.

Reggie went on for about two minutes, screaming at George about the way he disrespected him. George just kept trying to get Reggie to calm down and get out of his face. Willie Randolph and I also tried to get Reggie to sit down. Finally we steered Reggie into the seat where I had been sitting, away from the aisle. I sat down next to him and kept my hand on his knee.

Reggie had overreacted, and he knew it. It was something he shouldn't have done. This was my only peek into what the old battling Yankees of the 1970s and 1980s must have been like. Obviously, there was a lot of history that went into that confrontation. George is uneasy with Reggie's clout with the media. It's tough to take on Reggie in the newspapers and expect to win. I don't think George likes negative press that involves him and the Yankees. He's very sensitive to that stuff.

I love Reggie. I got to know him well when we were broadcasters together with the Angels in 1990. Reggie is the kind of guy who can offend people if you don't know him. He's a lot deeper than people think. He's a very sensitive person who, by the way he gets on people, sometimes doesn't think other people are sensitive.

Handling Reggie is a full-time job. He has a good eye for talent, and he has great knowledge and insights to share with my players, but sometimes he overloads them. It's not that what he says isn't good, but enough is enough. I liked having him around because he tells you what he thinks of players and situations. Reggie thinks he can detect fear in a person, almost like a dog's instinct to do that. He'd tell me, "I don't like the way this guy is walking around. I don't like his look." Then I'd go see for myself. I'd talk to that player and make my own judgment. Sometimes I'd come back to Reggie and say, "I think you're wrong," and he was fine with that. He didn't try to talk me into his way of thinking. One of the things I like best about Reggie is that he's been to the World Series and proved to be a clutch performer. I want to be surrounded by as many of those people as possible. When you watch from the stands or on television, you have no idea what's going on in the stomachs of the people on the field in that kind of pressure. I wasn't intimidated at all having Reggie around. It's comforting to be around people who've been in the foxhole.

We managed to make it to Texas without further incident. Later that day I ran into the maid as she was cleaning my hotel room. She noticed my Yankees suitcase and asked, "Are you with the team?" I said, "Yes, I'm the manager." She smiled and said, "Oh, yes. You're the one who sits next to that round guy." I guess Zim was becoming a cult hero.

When I arrived at the ballpark that night, Jose Cardenal gave me a plastic bag full of hot peppers. Jose has friends all over the world, and he told me these came from Mexico. He knows I like hot peppers. I thanked him and said, "Hope they bring me luck."

Jimmy Key pitched a gutsy ball game, but he wasn't getting the calls to go his way. When I took him out after five innings, he had thrown 101 pitches and we were trailing 2–1. I turned the ball over to Nelson. Nellie was terrific, shutting down that powerful Rangers lineup with three shutout innings. As I watched him mow down Texas, I smiled, thinking how good I felt about my decision to let him get the last out of our division-clinching game.

We were three outs away from losing when—who else?—Jeter started a rally in the ninth inning. He advanced to third on a single by Raines and scored the tying run when Bernie hit a sacrifice fly. Three batters later, Mariano Duncan knocked in Raines with a single to give us a 3–2 lead. Wetteland took care of the ninth inning to put us one win away from the American League Championship Series.

After that game I went out to eat with my wife and some friends. People were lined up to get into the restaurant, so they sneaked us in through a back door to seat us. And who happened to be seated at the next booth? Jeter. The kid was everywhere. The people at the restaurant were great. They wished us luck and talked about how happy they were to have the Rangers in the playoffs for the first time. It was hard for their players not to feel the same way. The first time you get in, it's huge. But when you play for the Yankees, the first plateau is nothing. That's like waking up in the morning. Even though the Yankees had not been to the World Series in eighteen years, the fans and the media made it clear they expected us to get there. That's why I was eager to close out the series the next day.

Rogers, who had played for Texas before he signed as a free agent after the 1995 season, started Game Four. I knew he was in trouble before the game, when he came back from warming up in the bullpen with Mel Stottlemyre.

"The fans were killing him out there," Mel said. "They were taunting him and screaming obscenities at him."

"What did Kenny do?" I asked.

"He motioned to one of the fans and said, 'That's my neighbor up there,' " Mel said.

I didn't like the sound of that. Kenny was trying to make light of the situation instead of being mentally tough and blocking it out. He lasted only two innings. We fell behind 4–0 but rallied once again, with the help of two home runs from Bernie Williams, to win 6–4. I got choked up in the dugout after the last out and cried. That was such an important series for us because if we had lost it, people would not have known that we existed. When I sat down at the traditional postgame press conference, I saw my wife standing in the back of the interview room with Arthur Sando, my friend from New York, and Bob and Kate Devlin, friends from Houston who had flown in for the game. That really made me emotional, seeing how happy Ali looked. After years of hiding my emotions and guarding my feelings, here I was getting choked up in front of cameras and reporters. I couldn't help it. It felt great. And then Bernie walked in, and I grew emotional all over again. Bernie was playing like the star I knew he was. Watching him play at that level was like watching one of my own children talk or walk for the first time.

Before we left Texas, I made sure to pack the hot peppers in my baseball equipment bag. And I made sure to say something to Williams. "Bernie," I said, "I'm going to have to pay *more* money to watch you play the next series."

When Yankee Stadium filled up with 56,495 people for Game One of the American League Championship Series against Baltimore, I told Bernie, "Look at this place. All these people are here to see you." He smiled.

For the fourth straight game we rallied to victory after trailing as late as the seventh inning. Mr. Rally himself, Jeter, tied the game with one out in the eighth inning with one of the most unforgettable and controversial home runs of all time. A twelve-year-old kid playing hooky from school reached over the right-field wall and pulled Jeter's fly ball into the stands. The Orioles right fielder, Tony Tarasco, had thought he was about to catch it, to put Baltimore four outs away from a victory. Instead, we went on to win 5–4, when Bernie delighted the packed house with a long home run in the eleventh inning. I was three wins away from the World Series.

I don't blame the kid for reaching out to catch Jeter's fly ball. I would have done the same thing at that age. What bothered me was that the media turned him into a hero. There's no doubt that Richie Garcia, the umpire who awarded Derek the home run, missed the call. I'm not sure if Tarasco would have caught the ball, so maybe Garcia should have ruled a double. But that's just one of those weird things that happen in baseball sometimes— like Nippy Jones getting hit on the foot in the 1957 World Series. That in itself didn't decide the game. My sisters and my wife preferred to think of Jeter's home run as more divine than weird. Rocco, they said, was our angel in the outfield. Who could argue? Jeter's home run had come in the same ballpark and exactly thirty-nine years to the day that my brother Frank hit his home run in Game Six of the 1957 World Series.

We lost Game Two 5–3, when Nellie gave up a two-run home run to Rafael Palmeiro in the seventh inning. I beat myself up pretty good over that, because I should have talked to Nellie before that at bat. Jeff had first base open, so he didn't have to throw a strike, especially when the count was three-and-one. He tried to throw a strike with a backdoor slider, the same pitch Kirk Gibson hit for his famous home run off Dennis Eckersley in the 1988 World Series. When a batter is hitting with a runner at second base with the game tied or his team down by one run, as Palmeiro and Gibson were, he's thinking about hitting the ball through the middle for a single. When you have that approach, you wait on the ball for a long time. And if the pitcher throws you a breaking ball, it seems as if the ball just stops for you. You wait all day for that ball, which is how you hit home runs: by not jumping at it.

As I packed after the game to go to Baltimore, I

said to myself, Well, I've got to pack the peppers. With each passing day the peppers were getting more rancid. They were starting to ooze fluid. I thought, I hope to hell this plastic bag doesn't break open in my bag.

Before Game Three at Camden Yards in Baltimore, I saw Orioles third baseman Todd Zeile during batting practice. Todd, who had played for me in St. Louis, had hit a home run in Game Two. In feint anger I yelled at Zeile, "I've been waiting my whole life to get to the World Series! You've got plenty of time!" After we won the pennant, Todd sent me a telegram. It said, "I'm still young. Congratulations."

We rallied again in Baltimore. Mike Mussina, the Orioles' best pitcher, was four outs away from beating us 2–1, when we erupted for four runs in a span of four batters. Who started the rally with two outs and nobody on in the eighth? Jeter, of course. The tie-breaking run was scored on a bizarre error by Zeile, who spiked the ball into the ground when he tried to stop his throwing motion suddenly, after changing his mind about making a throw to second base. As the ball rolled away, Bernie alertly dashed home. We were ahead two games to one. I was two wins away from the World Series.

I was getting anxious about being so close to realizing my dream. I also knew we were 7–0 in Baltimore against the Orioles. How much longer could that streak continue? All my life Rocco had been a calming presence for me. And that night in my hotel room was no different. Rocco visited me in a dream. It was the first time I had dreamed about him since he passed away four months earlier. I dreamed that I heard a knock at my door. I opened it, and there stood Rocco. He didn't say a word. He just smiled in a peaceful, contented kind of way. I'll never forget that look on his face. I knew my dead brother was telling me something. He was telling me that everything was going to be all right.

We won Game Four without having to stage another comeback, 8–4. I was one victory away from the World Series. I was very determined the next day to close it out, but I was also extremely nervous. Pettitte, who had struggled in his previous two playoff outings, was my starting pitcher. I told Jimmy Leyritz, the catcher that day, "Make sure you use the fastball. Don't fall in love with that cut fastball." Andy's youth had showed in his previous two starts; he thought he had to pitch differently in the postseason than in the regular season. Jimmy called a great game, and Pettitte, staked to an early 6–0 lead, pitched superbly for eight innings. Wetteland pitched the ninth.

At 7:20 P.M. on October 13, 1996, Cal Ripken, who was born one month and one day before my debut in the major leagues, hit a ground ball to Jeter. Derek threw the baseball in the dirt to first base to Tino Martinez, who made a great play to catch it for the final out of a 6–4 victory. Thirty-six years and 4,272 games since I put on a major league uniform for the first time, my dream had come true. Joseph Paul Torre finally was going to the World Series.

In my mind's eye I visualized where my wife and sisters were sitting in the stands. I thought about Frank in his hospital bed in New York. I thought about Rocco and felt his presence with me. I thought about all my friends who encouraged me to never give up my dream. A great, powerful wave of emotion just washed over me. It overwhelmed me. I cried, knowing what a fortunate man I was. I was truly loved by family and friends who wanted this for me even more than I wanted it for myself.

Then Reggie Jackson embraced me and whispered, "I'm happy for you." And then I totally lost it. I started bawling, because I knew that Reggie, this strong man who has been accused of being into himself so much, meant it from his heart.

I didn't go on the field. The celebration belonged to the players. It was more satisfying for me to watch it rather than be mobbed in the middle of it. I thanked each of my players as they made their way through the dugout to the clubhouse. By the time I got inside, my family was waiting for me in the manager's office. I hugged my wife and baby tightly, and I saw the look of surprise on Ali's face at the way I completely broke down. She had never seen me cry so openly. After the Texas victory I did a decent job holding back many of the tears. But during the celebration in Baltimore they flowed freely. Then George called with congratulations, crying with happiness as he struggled for the right words. "You did a great job," he said, leaving out his usual "but we have more work to do." We had done everything we needed to do, and he knew it. A bit later the reporter for NBC, Jim Gray, asked me about Rocco. I didn't expect that question. And it started me crying all over again. Ali said I hadn't had time to grieve for Rocco during the season. She may be right. I guess I kept my deepest emotions about Rocco's death locked behind my responsibility to my players and the Yankees organization. But getting to the World Series caused me to let down my guard, and when I did, the sadness of losing a brother I loved and admired overpowered me.

I cried many years' worth of tears that day in Baltimore. (I did, however, remember to bring the peppers back to New York.) I felt so fortunate to be supported by so many loving people, including all of Ali's fifteen siblings and their spouses, which, including their children, is my midwestern fan club in itself: her brothers John, David, Michael, Preacher and his wife, Nancy, Jimmy and Jan, Joe and Gina, Mark and Cheryl, Larry and Sharlene, Stan and Peggy, and her sisters Judy, Katie, Rosie and her husband Butch Putnick, Mary and Gary Even, Diane and Steve Bierman, and Lucy and Steve Borchers. And then, as if every last drop of water had burst forth from behind a dam, there were no more left. I stopped crying. I had reached my dream. Winning the World Series was the cherry on top of my hot fudge sundae. The pressure was off, and I was going to have fun being there. It's like all the athletes who go through years of training and several rounds of trials just to make the Olympic team. When they finally make the team, it's an honor in itself to be there and represent their country. I felt the same way about the World Series. And it was more fun that I ever could have imagined.

We waited to find out who would be our opponent. Either way, I would be facing one of my former teams, the Cardinals or the Braves. I didn't have a preference, though the Braves were the defending champions, and you always want to play the best. When that National League Championship Series went to a seventh game, I didn't watch. We had a team party that night at the Manhattan restaurant owned by my friend Joe Ponte. There was nothing I could do about that game in St. Louis. I preferred to enjoy the food and the company. Atlanta blew open that game very early. For the first time since I was a teenager watching Frank in his uniform number 14, the World Series would match the Yankees against the Braves.

On October 20, in front of 56,365 fans, Bob Sheppard, the voice of Yankee Stadium, introduced me before Game One of the World Series. I had one thought on my mind as I ran from the dugout to the first-base line: Don't trip. Reggie Jackson and Yogi Berra, two of the greatest World Series stars ever, had warned me that being introduced would be an emotionally powerful experience. It was even more emotional than I expected. A loud ovation shook the stadium. I had goose bumps on my arms. I looked up at the scoreboard in left field, and for the first time in my life I saw that no other games were being played or scheduled. I was at the center of the major league baseball universe. The excitement was incredible. All my years of dreaming about it didn't prepare me for the thrill of being introduced in a World Series. When I heard the crowd I knew I wasn't dreaming anymore. It was real. I was a little bit nervous, but more than anything I was thrilled to be there. When the game began, with Pettitte's first pitch, I was the happiest man alive. Normally I don't get caught up in the surroundings of the game. But on that first pitch I noticed a spectacular light show of hundreds of flashbulbs popping in the night all around the old ballpark. And for the rest of the night it was all downhill from there.

The Braves destroyed us 12–1. Atlanta rookie Andruw Jones, whose thirty-one career games were just slightly fewer than what it had taken me to get to the World Series, ripped two home runs. What bothered me was that both pitches Jones hit out of the park were up. Our scouts had specifically said he likes the ball up. Our pitchers made several mistakes like that. I met with some of my pitchers and catchers before the next game to emphasize the importance of our scouting reports. My players didn't know much about the Braves, but our scouts who had been watching them for a month did. We had to do a better job of relying on the reports.

Before Game Two the next night Bob Watson addressed the team. He told the players that he hadn't yet thanked them for the job they did all year and that he was immensely proud of them. I thought Bob sounded a little too much like he was delivering a eulogy, which is understandable because he had been listening to George all day. George can be very pessimistic. He likes to prepare himself for the worst. After listening to Bob, I decided I ought to say something as well.

"Listen," I said, "we've played and beaten better offensive teams than Atlanta—beat them with regularity. I'm talking about Cleveland, Baltimore, Texas. . . . There's no reason why we can't beat this team."

Deep down, though, I knew we were in trouble that night. Greg Maddux, the master magician, was pitching for Atlanta, and we still had rust on our bats after sitting out the five days since beating Baltimore. Steinbrenner walked into my office about ninety minutes before the first pitch, and said, "This is a must game." I barely looked up at him, and said nonchalantly, "You should be prepared for us to lose again tonight. But then we're going to Atlanta. Atlanta's my town. We'll take three games there and win it back here on Saturday."

George looked at me like I had two heads. He didn't say anything. He was dumbfounded.

Maddux threw a gem in Game Two, beating us 4–0. He's like a right-handed Whitey Ford—he dominates a game without being overpowering. We had lost the first two games of the World Series by a combined score of 16–1, the worst such showing among all ninety-two World Series ever played. There was only one thing to do: bring the peppers to Atlanta. A light drizzle was falling as I made the short walk from the exit gate at Yankee Stadium to the team buses that would take us to the airport and our charter flight to Atlanta. I actually felt good about going on the road. Not only had the six off days taken the edge off our game, but we also looked like a distracted team at home. The players hadn't gotten their World Series tickets until Friday, the day before the opener was rained out. Dealing with a constant barrage of ticket requests from friends and family can be a headache. Moreover, the pressure had been squarely on our shoulders at home. We felt like we had to hurry and get a win or two under our belts before going on the road. We didn't look loose because of that. Now we were back to being the underdogs in a hostile environment. I liked my team under those conditions.

Small crowds of fans waited in the rain behind police barricades that had been set up for our walk to the buses. They started chanting, "Bring it back! Bring it back!" I smiled and thought, We will.

At about three o'clock in the afternoon, five hours before Game Three began, I was sitting at the desk in the manager's office of the visiting clubhouse at Atlanta Fulton County Stadium. I happened to be taking care of some very important advance work for the game—I was trying to come up with World Series tickets. It seemed like there was no end to the number of people I knew who needed tickets to watch my club, the New York Yankees, play the Atlanta Braves. Every so often I'd call Bill Acree, the Braves' traveling secretary, and say, "Billy, I need four tickets." And then I'd write him a check and send one of the clubhouse attendants to run it up to his office. A little while later I'd get a call from someone else who wanted tickets, and I'd go through the same routine with Bill.

In between the phone calls and the check writing, I'd try to stay relaxed by doing a little self-hypnosis, just clearing my mind as I sat alone in the small office. When I was manager of the Mets, Father Joe Dispenza, a priest who traveled with us, taught me relaxation techniques. With that team a manager needed all the spiritual and mental help he could get. Now, outside my door in the main clubhouse, my coaches and players were also getting ready for what was a must-win game for us. My players were as loose as always; a bunch of them were engaged in a putting competition on the clubhouse carpet. Then my telephone rang.

"I have a phone call for Mr. Torre from a Mr. Steelbredder," the operator said. "Will you take the call?"

"Yeah, I'll take it," I told the stadium operator. I wasn't sure if it was actually George or not. I used to get crank calls during the season from jokesters who thought it was funny to call me up pretending to be George. About halfway through the season I started checking into hotels under the fictitious name Joe Russo—it was Italian and short, and people knew how to spell it. The calls stopped.

When George did come on the line, I could tell it was really him. That's because he doesn't say hello on the telephone. He just starts talking. I guess he's not interested in wasting even a second of his time.

"We can't be embarrassed," he said. That's one of George's favorite words: *embarrassed.* He uses it all the time. "We had the city to ourselves. New York was our town. But if we lose this thing, we're going to lose the city too. Let's not get embarrassed. Because I'll tell you one thing, Joe: If we lose, everything we've done up until now won't mean a damned thing. All that we've accomplished won't mean anything."

"Well, I don't think so, George, but don't worry about it," I said. "We're fine. We're fine."

"I hope you're right," he said. "I trust you."

I've always had the capacity to calm George. I talked to him the way I did my nervous troops back in basic training in 1962, when I was in the Air National Guard at Lackland Air Force Base in Texas. That was during the Cuban missile crisis. I was put in charge of about fifty guys—I guess because I had some leadership skills being a major league player, though I think being one of the biggest guys there helped too. We were on a march one night when my troops started moaning about going to war. So I said to them, "Don't worry. We're not going to war." I figured, what the hell could they tell me if I was wrong: "We told you we were going to war"? You might as well tell them, "Don't worry, we're not going." If you're right, everybody thinks you're real smart. And if you're wrong, nobody really cares, because by then they have too many things to worry about.

More than anything, I think George wanted us to avoid the embarrassment of getting swept. I don't think he was thinking about winning the World Series at that point. I found out after the Series that a few hours before he called me, he had traveled by himself to Atlanta on a flight from La-Guardia Airport. As he walked down the jetway to his first-class seat, he struck up a conversation with a writer he had known for years. "This series reminds me of 'seventy-six, when we got swept by the Reds," Steinbrenner said. "But we came back and won two world championships after that. Atlanta's a great team. They're the defending champions. You have to tip your cap to them. There's no shame in losing to a club like that."

Naturally, George didn't exactly leave our conversation at "I trust you." He had some recommendations about my lineup for the game that night against Tom Glavine, the Braves' left-handed pitcher. He asked me about playing Strawberry in right field instead of O'Neill. I had already decided to make that switch. O'Neill had been bothered for weeks by a pulled leg muscle, and in those first two games he didn't look to me like he had swung the bat with much authority. George also suggested the idea of using Fielder at first base instead of Martinez, which was another move I had already decided to make. I couldn't play both of them because we didn't have use of the designated hitter in Atlanta; you play under National League rules in the World Series when the National League team is home. Cecil had had base hits in his last two at bats in Game Two, while Tino had not driven in a run the entire postseason. It looked to me like he was pressing.

Then George said to me, "What about Kenny Rogers? Is there anyone else?" He was already worried about my Game Four pitcher.

"I could come back with Pettitte tomorrow on two days' rest," I said, aware that Pettitte had thrown only fifty-five pitches before his third-inning exit in Game One. "But if I do that, then I'm still going to need a pitcher for Game Five. And if I use Rogers there, his confidence will be totally shot because I've just bumped him from starting Game Four. Don't worry about Rogers, George. We've won every game he's pitched in the postseason. He's pitching tomorrow. He'll be fine. Don't worry."

"Okay, I trust you," George said. We talked for another minute or so again about my lineup, and that was it. George, as he usually does, hung up without saying good-bye.

I was glad to have David Cone as my starting pitcher that night. I knew he had pitched in Atlanta before and would not pitch defensively in that small ballpark. I had held him out until Game Three because I wanted my left-handers, Pettitte and Key, pitching in Yankee Stadium in the first two games. Left-handers have a history of pitching better than right-handers at the stadium because they can take the short right-field porch out of play by matching up better against left-handed hitters. Atlanta was a weaker offensive club against left-handers anyway. I also used that order of pitchers because I knew that Game Three can often be a pivotal game in a series, and Cone is a great big-game pitcher. That's the very reason we signed him as a free agent in the first place: to pitch crucial games like this.

I remember on the eve of the World Series telling Pettitte, Key, and Cone their assignments. Jimmy looked surprised that he would start Game Two ahead of Cone. But David just told me, "I had a feeling you might go this way." A lot of my decisions worked out in my favor over the course of the World Series, but deciding to pitch David in Game Three was probably the best decision I made.

I also knew that as long as we kept the game close, especially if we had a lead in the middle innings, we would win. All I thought about was winning that night. If you think about the magnitude of the overall task ahead of us—we had to win four times in no more than six games with Tom Glavine, Denny Neagle, John Smoltz, and Greg Maddux pitching for the Braves with full rest—you would be overwhelmed. I didn't necessarily think about beating their great starting pitchers, but I wanted to get them out of the game so that we could get into their bullpen. I liked our chances against their middle relievers. You have to think small: get a lead, protect it, win one game, and then play the next game.

I had another reason why I still liked our chances, though no hard-bitten baseball man would dare include this on his scouting report: I believed I was managing a team with destiny on its side. We were 5–0 on the road in the postseason, an almost unheard-of testament of resolve. From Jeter's kid-glove home run to five comeback wins already in the postseason to Cardinal's stinky peppers, I had a feeling good things were happening for us.

It was very important for us to get a lead in Game Three. So when Tim Raines led off the game with a walk, I flashed the sign to my third-base coach, Willie Randolph, that I wanted Jeter to bunt for a base hit. I didn't want Derek to give himself up totally, but if he did bunt for a hit, I figured the worst thing that could happen would be he'd get thrown out and advance Raines to second base. That's exactly what happened, and when Bernie followed that bunt with a single to knock in Raines, I felt great. We had our first lead of the World Series.

We made it 2–0 in the fourth, when we turned a leadoff error by Braves shortstop Jeff Blauser into a run.

Cone was magnificent. He had a three-hit shutout through five innings. I knew that if he could protect the lead through one more inning, our chances of winning were about as good as they get. We were 70–3 during the regular season whenever we had a lead after six innings. That's primarily because of the Formula. That's why the sixth inning was always the most important inning of our games. Cone needed to get us three more outs.

Bobby Cox, the Atlanta manager, allowed his pitcher, Glavine, to lead off the sixth inning. Cone committed a grave error: He walked the pitcher. Then Marquis Grissom singled. Mark Lemke tried to bunt but popped out. But then Cone walked Chipper Jones. I couldn't tell whether Cone suddenly was tiring—he had thrown only eighty-seven pitches, a low count for him—but somehow he had lost the command of his pitches. The bases were loaded. Fred McGriff, the Braves' hottest hitter, was the batter, with Ryan Klesko, another dangerous left-handed slugger, right behind him. I had a left-hander, Graeme Lloyd, ready in the bullpen.

The Braves were in position to blow us away. If they did break the game open—just one swing could do it—and take a three-games-to-none lead in the Series, well, even I would have to at least begin to question whether destiny had deserted us. I looked at the three runners on base and at McGriff walking to the plate, and I thought to myself, This is the whole World Series right here. If we don't stop them here, we just might get swept away.

I had a huge decision to make. Should I leave a struggling Cone in to pitch to McGriff, or should I play the percentages and bring in my left-hander, Lloyd? I turned to my bench coach, Don Zimmer, and said, "I'm going out there to the mound and see what he says."

As I left the dugout, I really didn't know what I was going to do. I jogged out to the mound. I didn't want Coney to think I had my mind made up to take him out. I had learned that lesson the hard way almost twenty years ago when I was managing the Mets. Jerry Koosman, a lefty, had been pitching a good game for us against Pittsburgh. We had a one-run lead. I had a right-handed pitcher warming in the bullpen. The Pirates had a right-handed hitter due up, but I knew they had John Milner, a good left-handed hitter, on their bench. So I walked slowly out to the mound, intending to tell Koosman that I wanted him to go ahead and pitch to the right-hander because I didn't want my right-handed reliever pitching to Milner. As soon as I got to the mound—and before I could say anything—Koosman reached out and handed me the ball. Shit, I thought. Now I had to take Koosman out of the game. He had effectively taken himself out, because he had convinced himself that he was out of the game by the way I walked to the mound. That made him lose his mental edge, and he was of no use anymore. After that I decided I would run to the mound whenever I just wanted to talk to the pitcher.

My gut feeling was that I wanted to leave Cone in the game. Cone is like Gibson, Koufax, and Maddux. They've earned the right to pitch in tough situations, no matter who's hitting. David has retired left-handed hitters his whole life. I hadn't kept him from pitching against the Braves just because they had McGriff. Now why all of a sudden should that make a difference? It would make a difference only if he was drained. What did he have left in his gas tank, if anything? I had to find out. And there was only one way to do it. I was going to stick my face as close as possible to his face and demand the truth out of him. I wanted to hear his words and look deep into his eyes.

"This is very important," I said to Cone, our eyes fixed on one another just inches apart. My catcher, Joe Girardi, was standing near us, but he might as well have been on the moon as far as I was concerned. It's never a good idea to ask the catcher about the pitcher while the pitcher is within earshot. You're unlikely to get an honest answer, because a pitcher will get angry at a catcher who says he's cooked. I told Cone, "I need the truth from you. How do you feel?"

"I'm okay," Cone said. "I lost the feel for my slider a little bit there, but I'm okay. I'll get this guy for you."

"This game is very important," I said. "I've got to know the truth, so don't bullshit me."

"I can get him," he said. "I can get out of this inning."

That was what I wanted to hear. And David didn't hesitate when he said it. But just as importantly, I liked the look I saw in his eyes. He was determined.

"Let's go get 'em," I said.

And then I left. I left the ball in Cone's hands. And I felt good about it. But I figured if McGriff got on base, I'd have to pull Cone.

David threw a strike to him, then got McGriff out on an infield pop-up for the second out of the sixth inning. That did it for me. Cone was fine, and so was I. This was his inning.

I spend a lot of my time trying to figure out what I can do better, and when things don't work, I really torture myself over them. But I felt good about this decision no matter what happened. Cone still had enough gas left. It was now a matter of execution. He then wavered a bit, walking Klesko to force in a run. It was a one-run game, 2–1, and Javy Lopez was batting for Atlanta. Cone responded. Lopez popped up an 0–1 pitch, and when Girardi squeezed it in foul ground, I knew the tide of the World Series had turned. Rivera and Wetteland, with two outs of help from Lloyd in between, nailed down what ended up a 5–2 victory. John gave me the ball from the last out, knowing it was my first World Series win.

All of a sudden, after serving as little more than bad props to the mighty Braves for two games, we were credible. We had some momentum. It's a good thing Coney pitched us through that sixth inning, because we played a courageous, historic game the next night that could only have happened with a win already under our belts. Game Four will go down in history as one of the most memorable World Series games ever and the signature game of the 1996 Yankees. But if Game Four had been Game Three—when we had yet to hold even a lead over the Braves—we could not have won it.

CHAPTER 9

Bulletproof

I FELT GREAT THE MORNING I WOKE UP before Game Four. I knew winning one game in the World Series could easily turn into a second win—and then you'd be rolling. I don't think that applies to the regular season, but momentum seems much more important in the postseason. That's why I felt a lot of pressure in Game Five of the American League Championship Series in Baltimore. If we had let the Orioles up off the floor with a win there, who knew what would happen afterward? You can't put the other team back on the offensive. That's exactly what the Braves had done, though, when they failed to break out against David Cone with the bases loaded in that critical sixth inning of Game Three. They let us back in the Series, and we came charging back with confidence when they did.

I also felt relaxed before Game Four because I had no major decisions to make about the lineup. We had beaten Tom Glavine, a left-hander, the night before with Wade Boggs, Tino Martinez, and Paul O'Neill on the bench in favor of Charlie Hayes, Cecil Fielder, and Darryl Strawberry. Atlanta was using another left-hander, Denny Neagle, in Game Four, so I wasn't about to change the lineup. The heat was off me. I'll admit, though, it did seem a little strange to be playing in the World Series with three guys in the middle of my lineup who hadn't even been with the club before the Fourth of July. It bothered me a little bit to be taking people out of the lineup who had been there all year. I reminded myself, though, that when you get to the World Series, you can't be concerned about reputation or hurting feelings. You have to decide who's going to help you win that day, which ultimately benefits everybody.

I had talked with Wade, Tino, and Paulie before Game Three—I didn't have to explain anything to them before Game Four because it was obvious I'd use the same lineup—and they handled it like professionals. Tino, however, looked more upset than the other guys. I think he was frustrated because he was having a bad postseason. He struggled because he fights himself so much. He wears himself out. He doesn't like you to say too much to him, either, so I stayed away from giving him any one-on-one advice. When I would see him walking by, though, I'd say something to somebody else loud enough that he could hear me. For instance, I'd grab O'Neill if I saw Tino next to him and say something like "Paulie, with this pitcher you have to . . ."

I felt the confidence in the clubhouse, too, before Game Four. The guys were pretty loose the whole time, even after that ass kicking in Game One. But it's amazing what one victory can do for you, especially when you're playing the world champs and you're the underdog. Bernie Williams was happy because a shipment of his bats had arrived from New York. Bernie had forgotten to pack them after Game Two for our trip to Atlanta. How do you forget your bats for the World Series? That's Bernie, though. He's an intelligent guy, but he's so oblivious to pressure and his surroundings that sometimes I think he doesn't even know what planet he's on. Bernie had borrowed Joe Girardi's bat for Game Three and hit a home run with it. But he still switched back to his own bats before Game Four.

Speaking of forgetting things, no one on our club remembered to bring to Atlanta the generic blue visiting lineup cards. Most clubs stock them in the visiting manager's office, anyway. But the only cards in my desk at Atlanta Fulton County Stadium were left behind by the Reds. The cards had CINCINNATI printed in boldface on top. It would have to do. I scratched out CINCINNATI, though it remained legible on my carbon copy. And that's the reason the greatest game I ever managed is recorded with a Cincinnati Reds lineup card. By the end of the night, that lineup card looked more unkempt than I do if I skip a day of shaving. As I use players, I scratch their names off a list on the right side of my card. Every player's name eventually would be crossed out that night except three: Andy Pettitte, who was my starting pitcher the next night, and starting pitchers Jimmy Key and David Cone, both of whom I came so close to using in the late innings that I had to tell them to change out of their soft-soled shoes, which starters typically wear when they're not pitching, and into their spikes.

I kept that lineup card, as I did all the others from the World Series. It's a thing of beauty. It seemed like every move I made, no matter how strange it might have looked to others, turned out right. Game Four will go down as a classic. I believe it's the signature game of the 1996 Yankees because it showcased our greatest strengths: our bullpen, our depth, and above all, our heart. It was the second-greatest comeback in World Series history and a perfect example of why anybody who thinks baseball with the designated hitter is better is nuts. Having the pitcher bat presents the manager with a major decision every time his turn comes up. It was great being back in the National League. I used ten players just in the ninth spot alone in the batting order. Game Four ended at 12:36 in the morning after four hours and seventeen minutes of excruciating drama—the longest of the 543 World Series games ever played. It included so many strategic twists—and here I'll give

CHASING THE DREAM

you an inside look at the best of them—that I'm
convinced a manager without National League experience could not have won it.

Kenny Rogers was my starting pitcher, a circum-
stance made possible by an act of God. No, Sister
Marguerite had nothing to do with it. He started
only because we had lost the first scheduled off-day,
due to the rainstorm that postponed Game One. In
fact, on the night of that rainout, I had petitioned
acting commissioner Bud Selig to keep the off-day
between Games Two and Three and drop the one
between Games Five and Six.

"Bud," I told him, "if you're going to give an
off-day, I'd rather have the first one—only because
the Braves had an opportunity to work out here at
Yankee Stadium. We should have the same opportunity to work out at their place. Let's even the
playing field."

"It makes sense," Selig said. "I'll think about it
and get back to you."

I didn't hear from him again about it. Bud had
been much easier to bargain with when he sold me
that 1960 Thunderbird. The rainout was a real dis-
advantage for us. If we had had the two off-days,
Rogers would not have been my Game Four starter.
I would have used Pettitte on short rest. So Rogers
got the call in a matchup against Neagle, who had
been pitching much better for the Braves lately
than he did after his trade from Pittsburgh, August
28. I told a couple of people before the game, "This

247

is a game we're going to have to win 8–6, 10–9, something like that."

I just thought, the way Kenny had been pitching, it would be a high-scoring game. Also, the previous day Rogers had bagged the traditional press conference featuring the next day's starting pitchers. Rick Cerrone, our director of media relations, came to me and said, "Kenny doesn't want to talk to the press."

"Fine," I told him. "Just tell the writers I think it's a good idea, so it can take some of the pressure off him."

But then I learned that Kenny was just kidding with Rick. By then it was too late to put the press conference together, so Rick announced during the game that Rogers would be available to the media after the game. I just let it go and didn't talk to Kenny about it. That's Kenny. He's one of the most difficult players to read that I've ever managed. But I don't put him in that Ed Whitson category, the kind of guy who can't pitch in New York. He just needs more confidence in himself.

Several times during the season Kenny would come into my office, and I had no idea what he was talking about. I guess he was reading the newspapers and people were writing that I didn't like him and that he was in my doghouse and things like that. So he'd ask me questions about my confidence in him or lack of it. I'd tell him, "Kenny, I know your equipment. I know your stuff. But it doesn't do me any good to believe in you unless you believe in yourself."

Sports medicine is an amazingly advanced field. But with Rogers I wish they could invent some procedure to transfer confidence. Hook up some device to his left arm and just inject it. At least that way I would have felt, going into Game Four, that we were going to be all right. Instead, I felt like with Kenny pitching, we would have to knock their starter out of the game in order to win.

I noticed an omen about Rogers right from the start. When Tim Raines led off for us in the first inning, Rogers still was throwing in the bullpen. That's never a good sign. All that means is you're not loose. There's a certain tightness a player gets before a big game—which is fine. In the past players never admitted to the fact that they got nervous and jumpy. It's okay to admit it now, but not back when I played. You were a man, and you weren't supposed to be nervous. Consider the word *bravery*. It's contingent upon being nervous and afraid. If you're not afraid, there's no reason to be brave. It's what you do in spite of not feeling right that makes you brave.

Kenny, though, could not seem to conquer his anxiety. After Neagle set us down in order, Rogers fell behind on the count on his first three hitters. Zimmer turned to me and barked, "He won't throw strikes!" Rogers, though, did get a ground-ball out from each of those hitters. Whenever a pitcher is getting ground-ball outs, I'm happy. It means he's getting his pitches down, which makes it more difficult for a batter to get good wood on the ball.

Kenny wasn't so fortunate in the second inning. He fell behind Fred McGriff, three-and-one. Then McGriff launched a bomb over the center-field wall. Now, home runs to center field or the opposite field don't bother me. You can't put the total blame on the pitcher for those. If a pitcher flat out makes a mistake, such as hanging a curveball or grooving a fastball down the middle, a hitter is going to pull it. But if the hitter goes the other way or to dead center with a pitch, you just tip your hat to the hitter. And if you do give up dingers, you want to give them up with nobody on base. Kenny, though, obviously was shell-shocked after that blast. He went into his four-corner defense and refused to throw a strike. That's what drives me nuts more than anything. You can't be afraid to throw strikes. That's not giving yourself or your team a chance. After he walked Javy Lopez, I turned to Zimmer and said, "Shit. I better talk to him." My mission: Pump up Kenny's deflated ego.

Sometimes I can light a fire under a pitcher by challenging his manhood—really cursing him out and asking him to show me some guts. With Kenny I have to be a little more careful. He was still an enigma to me. As I walked to the mound, I decided to be firm with him but be careful not to go overboard. I didn't want to crush his confidence; I wanted to rebuild it.

"Listen, you threw the ball really well in the first

inning," I told him. "Now, because of the home run, you want to start guiding the ball, and you're afraid to throw strikes. You've got to be the same guy you were last inning and throw strikes. You've got good shit. Don't be afraid to challenge people. Now let's go!"

Kenny didn't say anything. He just nodded. So what happened? He walked Andruw Jones. Now he really ticked me off. He had developed a mindset that he was not going to throw strikes. Your good pitchers don't throw strikes, but they throw pitches that *look* like strikes. Maddux is a master at that. Tom Seaver used the expression "pitching around the strike zone."

Rogers fell behind another batter, Jermaine Dye, but he did get an out on a fly ball long enough to advance both runners one base. With Jeff Blauser batting, I thought that Cox might squeeze in that situation, even if our scouting reports on the Braves said he didn't use the squeeze play. I knew better than that. I remember one game I managed against him in St. Louis when I called for three straight pitch-outs, with Rafael Belliard batting. On the third one Cox did have the squeeze play on, and we got the runner.

This time, though, Rogers was having such a tough time throwing strikes that I didn't want to pitch out. And if they did squeeze, big deal. This early in the game, I was willing to trade a run for an out. That time Cox squeezed with Belliard, it was late in the game, when one run is as good as five. It was only the second inning here. I'd take two outs and two runs in.

Sure enough, Blauser put down a bunt on a two-and-one count, and Lopez jogged home. The worst part of the play was that we didn't get an out. Mariano Duncan, my second baseman, failed to cover first base. He broke toward second because Jones was running on the pitch from first base. I couldn't get mad at Duncan about that; you don't want the shortstop covering second base with a pull hitter up. But that's why they say you never stop learning in baseball. We'll address that very play in spring training. The only thing a second baseman can do there to prevent leaving first base uncovered is to check the runner at third before breaking toward second base. If the guy on third is running, the second baseman has to get to first. You should react to the runner on third, not the one on first.

Neagle also bunted, sending Blauser to second, with Jones holding at third. Then Grissom smoked a double past Derek Jeter, making the score 4–0. Later on some writers asked me why didn't I walk Grissom to pitch to Lemke. Hey, I second-guessed myself when he got the hit, but analyzing it later, he hit the ball on the ground—hard, but on the ground. And that's what I wanted to see out of Kenny. When he's pitching well, he'll get a lot of ground balls because of the sink on his pitches. Anyway, I hate to walk people intentionally early in the game. You're just asking for trouble.

Rogers did get Lemke on a grounder, to temporarily stop the bleeding. He also managed our first hit off Neagle, a single in the third. Standing on first base, Rogers said to my coach, Jose Cardenal, "I'm glad I can hit, because I'm not pitching very good." Cardenal told me about it between innings. I didn't think that was real funny. It's that false mentality, trying to make light of the situation. Even when you're kidding, there's still that negative thought in your head.

When Kenny allowed singles to Chipper Jones and McGriff to start the bottom of the third inning, I had to pull him. The one thing as a manager you have to stay away from is letting the game get blown out of shape. And I also had to remember that although Neagle is a good pitcher, he's not Maddux, Smoltz, or Glavine. We were still in this game. So I brought in Brian Boehringer. As Kenny left the field, I still felt the same way about him: I'm a Kenny Rogers fan. The problem is, he isn't.

Boehringer did a fine job, getting outs from all six batters he faced—one of those outs, a sacrifice fly, made it 5–0—before I had to hit for him in the fifth with Luis Sojo. As well as Boehringer pitched, I had to put up a better hitter for him when we were down by five runs. In the American League, because the pitcher doesn't bat, I would have stayed with him as long as he was effective. I had confidence, too, in relievers David Weathers, who had pitched most of the year with the Florida Marlins, Jeff Nelson, and Graeme Lloyd. I would not use Mariano Rivera and John Wetteland if we were trailing by a lot, so I could keep them for a game we could win.

The Braves tacked on another run in the fifth against Weathers. Chipper Jones had walked, moved to second on a balk, and scored on a double by Andruw Jones that bounced off Hayes's glove. I never saw that balk. I happened to be looking down at the time. But of course, that didn't stop me from mounting what might have looked on television like a vigorous argument with Jerry Davis, the National League umpire working second base who made the call.

"What did he do?" I asked Davis as I made my way across the field.

"He started to come around with the ball in his hand and then stopped," Davis said.

"You know, Jerry," I argued, "the problem is, you see somebody new, and something in his motion looks funny to you."

"Uh, Joe, he was with Florida all year."

I immediately recognized the folly of my argument. Florida is a National League team, and Davis, an NL umpire, was very familiar with the former Marlins pitcher.

"You know, that's a good point, Jerry," I said. "You're right."

I promptly wheeled around and headed back to the dugout, doing my best to surpress a chuckle and hoping my face wasn't too red.

When my team came off the field after that fifth inning, I delivered a message to them as they gathered in the middle of the dugout. Okay, things didn't look great. Neagle was throwing a two-hit shutout, and we were trailing by six runs. No Yankee team had come from that far back to win a World Series game. Ever. Only one other club had ever mounted a bigger comeback in the history of the Fall Classic: Connie Mack's 1929 Philadelphia Athletics. On top of that, we were only nine outs away from being down three games to one in the series, a virtually insurmountable deficit against the kind of starting pitchers the Braves had. But if you think that way, you're beat. So I didn't say a word of it. I reminded the players to think small.

"Let's cut it in half right here," I told them. "Take small bites. Do the little things to get one run at a time. Let's put a little pressure on them."

As had happened so often in the season, especially in October, a rally began with the unflappable kid, Jeter. He plays every game, including the World Series, like it's Saturday morning on the sandlots of Marine Park. After the first playoff game against Texas, after he left six runners on, all the writers were asking me, "Are you going to talk to him?" I didn't see any reason to. He just hadn't gotten a big hit. So what? He didn't seem to act any differently. That's why it's important for a manager to walk through the clubhouse a lot—to sense anything. I find out a lot in the trainers' room. I can sense tension there. How? Strained conversation, a looseness, what they're doing when you walk in, or if your walking in affects anything.

Jeter, though, doesn't seem to ever change. And I hope he never does. He'll now have a lot of forces pushing him in different directions: his agents, the media, and of course, all the women. Keeping up his work habits will be the key. I'll notice right away this spring if he's changing. If he stops working, he'll have a problem.

What I like about Jeter as a hitter is, he uses the whole field. He became even more right-field conscious against the Braves because their whole damned pitching staff lives on the outside of the plate. Check out their outfield alignment sometime. They overshift more to the opposite field than any club I've ever seen, and they do it on everybody.

So naturally, Jeter hit a fly ball near the right-field line. Dye didn't seem to have a good line on the ball, but umpire Tim Welke didn't help his cause either. The umpire never made an effort to get out of Dye's way. Dye had to run around the umpire like a basketball defender trying to get around a pick. What should have been the first out dropped into foul territory. Given another swing, Jeter blooped a single in front of Dye.

I know that Cox beefed about Welke for the rest of the Series, calling it the turning point of Game Four. I don't know about that. I don't know if that was the umpire's fault. I guess he has to be out of the way, but he was looking at the two infielders coming at him. And that didn't turn the series around. Even after that ball landed foul, the Braves still were ahead 6–0 and Neagle still hadn't given up a hard hit. Welke had nothing to do with all the hits and walks that came after that.

For me, it was a good sign. We had come from behind so many times during the year, especially in the postseason, that whenever something as lucky as a misplayed pop-up went our way, I figured more breaks would follow. I just wanted to get into Atlanta's middle relief. Of course, I took for granted that our pitching was going to shut them down. That's the way you have to think. That's why, when you're managing a team like Detroit, with its raggedy pitching staff, it's tough to figure out how many runs you need. That's a helpless feeling.

So I never thought this game looked over. You can't lose sight of the fact that this is the World Series and there are only four games left to play. This is it. Jeter was as good as anybody feeling that we were never going to lose. I'd go out to change a pitcher, and he'd come to the mound and say, "We're going to win this game." I love that. If you say it enough, you believe it.

Neagle walked Bernie Williams, and now it looked like all of a sudden he was running out of gas. I had my big man up, Cecil Fielder, with runners at first and second. He's the kind of slugger who can cut the lead in half with one swing, but in this series Fielder suddenly became much more than a power hitter. He was simply a tough out, a guy who was really locked in.

Soon after we traded for Cecil, I had asked him about having a game plan when he went to the plate, including the thought of driving the ball to the opposite field. "I can't do that," he said. Cecil didn't want to think too much up at the plate; he just wanted to go up there and mash. But he had one at bat in August against Randy Johnson that stuck with me. Randy can blow his fastball past Cecil, especially if he gets it up. With two strikes, though, Cecil hit one of Johnson's heaters up the middle for a two-run single. That told me he knows what he's doing up there, even though he may not understand some of the things I was trying to tell him.

Cecil wound up with nine hits in the World Series: three to left field, three to center field, and three to right field. Now he collected one of those opposite-field hits against Neagle, drilling an outside pitch so hard to right field that it ate up Dye after one wicked bounce. As the ball bounced away from Dye, Derek and Bernie scored; third-base coach Willie Randolph made a terrific call in sending Williams home. I think Willie so surprised the Braves' defense by sending Bernie with no outs that Bernie scored without a throw to the plate.

Now it was 6–2, Cecil on second, and Charlie Hayes was up. His job was to get Cecil to third base. I can't tell you how proud I am of these guys because they never lost sight of what they had to do. Charlie did hit the ball to the right side—so well, in fact, that he wound up driving in Cecil with a single.

I was so pleasantly surprised about Charlie

Hayes. I had never been crazy about watching him play on other teams. I didn't like his body language on the field. I'd had chances to get him in trades before and said no thanks. Then on August 30 Bob Watson asked me if I had interest in Hayes. At that point Boggsy was struggling a little bit, so it was tempting. The guy who turned me around on Hayes was Jim Leyland, the Pirates' manager at the time. I called him up and asked him about Charlie. He said, "You'll love him, and he'll help you." He was right.

Just as I had asked the guys in my dugout meeting, we cut the lead in half. Now I was greedy and wanted more. Why not? When Darryl drew a walk off Terrell Wade, we once again had two on and nobody out.

Cox brought in Mike Bielecki, a right-hander whom Zimmer had managed once in Chicago. Do I pinch-hit for Duncan, who is one-for-eleven, with a left-handed hitter like Boggs? No way. Duncan came up with too many big hits for us all year. Besides, you just can't run yourself out of players. It's still only the sixth inning. You still have to manage the whole game. I remember a game I was playing with the Mets in Cincinnati. Joe Frazier was the manager. I was leading off the ninth inning when he pinch-hit for me with a left-handed hitter. The game ended with one of our pitchers, Skip Lockwood, hitting for himself with a couple of runners on because he had no players left. You really have to project what could happen, to think where you're going to need your players. That's especially true in the National League. In the American League you can't run out of players because of the designated hitter.

Do I ask Dunc to bunt? No way, again. I know Mariano is a lousy bunter. He's just not comfortable doing it, so I'm not going to ask him. So I let him hack. Mariano is such a freewheeling first-ball hitter that you could throw the resin bag up there and he'd swing at it. Bielecki struck him out.

I then decided to pinch-hit for Girardi, who was hitless in the series to that point, with O'Neill. I wasn't sure what Cox would do. If he had brought in a left-hander, Steve Avery, I would have sent Leyritz up. I think at that point Cox already was committed to bringing in his closer, Mark Wohlers, in the eighth inning. Why did I feel that way? I thought Cox felt the game was close to slipping away, and he didn't have anyone he trusted to pitch the eighth inning. Even if it meant Cox would not have Wohlers rested for Game Five, he wanted to be up three games to one. This had become a huge game for him because he had that big lead.

Bielecki was throwing gas. Zimmer told me, "I've never seen him throw this hard." He whiffed O'Neill and Tino Martinez, who batted for Weathers.

It was 6–3 then. Zim gave me a nudge. "Check out your sister," he said. I looked behind me in the field boxes, and there was Sister Marguerite dancing in the aisles. She was doing the macarena.

Then I asked Jeff Nelson to keep the Braves in check. He did a perfect job, keeping the game at 6–3 with two hitless innings, bringing us to an eighth-inning showdown with Wohlers. I heard later that Bobby Cox took some heat for pulling Bielecki, who looked like Nolan Ryan out there. But it was the right move—he had gotten out of Bielecki what he wanted. It used to be managers brought in their closer with a runner on second base, leaving the guy no breathing room. Now most managers prefer to give their horse the ball with a little room for error. I'm with Bobby on that one.

Hayes led off against Wohlers, and I couldn't afford to pinch-hit for him. I was down to Aldrete, Fox, and Boggs. If I led off with Boggs, who would I have to knock in the run? Fox? Aldrete? They weren't yet proven hitters in those clutch situations. I knew Boggs had trouble knocking in runs, but I still had to save him for that kind of situation. Plus, I was committed in my mind to starting Hayes the next day against Smoltz. But if he was going to play against Smoltz, why not use him against Wohlers?

Then something happened that made me think once again that this was meant to be. Hayes topped a ball down the third-base line. It clearly was rolling foul. It even crossed over onto the chalk line. But suddenly, amazingly, the damned thing took a right-hand turn. It wound up fair by more than a foot. It was so absurd that Charlie stood on first base laughing. Like Jeter's divine home run against the Orioles, it's easy to believe that Rocco had his hand in that hit as well. I admit that at that point I was thinking about destiny, that we were destined to win this thing. There's nothing wrong with thinking that way—you just have to make sure you don't get caught up in it to the point where you stop working. You have to continue to work at it. But that kind of thinking keeps you from getting anxious. You start saying, "Whatever's going to happen is going to happen, but it sure looks good for us."

Darryl came up with another hit, a single that put runners on first and second. And more good things happened for us. Duncan hit a smash to shortstop. It was a sure double-play ball, especially because Cox had put his defensive specialist, Belliard, in the game. Whoops! He couldn't handle the hop. Belliard did get an out at second base, but he lost the double play. "Wow," I said to myself. "I love this." Our whole dugout was buzzing with excitement. The dugouts in Atlanta Fulton County Stadium are terrible—the seats are way too low. So everybody was standing up or sitting on the front ledge of the dugout.

Leyritz was the batter, but I started to think about who should pinch-hit for Nelson, whose spot in the lineup was coming up next. Aldrete? Boggs? If Leyritz got on, it would be Boggs. If not, Aldrete. Jimmy had a pretty good hack at Wohlers's first pitch, a ninety-eight-mile-per-hour fastball, and fouled it back. Wohlers had this strange look on his face, one that said something like, "Wow, I just gave him my best bullet, and he was right on it." I thought Jimmy was slightly behind the ball, but the damage to Wohlers's psyche was done. He wasn't sure if he could get Leyritz out with his best heater. I thought about that time I pinch-hit for Jimmy and he was pissed off, telling me he was a better hitter in big situations.

After that, Wohlers tried to trick Jimmy with two breaking balls, neither of which was a strike. So Wohlers tried another fastball again, this one at ninety-nine miles per hour. And again Jimmy fouled it back. I still think that if Wohlers had thrown his fastball a little higher—at least as high as the belt—Jimmy wouldn't have been able to catch up to it. Wohlers has one of the best fastballs on earth. He is so intimidating with that heater that Leyritz decided to use Darryl Strawberry's bat against him; Jimmy had only a couple of his own bats left and was afraid of breaking them against Wohlers. Straw's bats were expendable. I found that to be pretty funny. I mean, it was the fourth game of the World Series. What was Jimmy saving his bats for?

After that second foul ball, Wohlers had seen enough. He said later that he thought Leyritz was "right on my fastball," so he eliminated the pitch from his thinking. With the count two-and-two, Wohlers threw a nasty slider, breaking it off down and away. Leyritz reached out and tapped the ball foul past third base. Sometimes great hitting isn't always about hitting home runs or putting the ball in play. Hank Aaron, for instance, was great at fouling off tough pitches to extend at bats. That's what Jimmy did. Wohlers decided to come back with another slider. If the previous one had been nasty, he tried to make this one even better. But when you try to do that, usually you wind up throwing a hanger, which is what Wohlers did. Jimmy connected solidly. I know how well the ball carries in the Launching Pad, and I've seen enough home runs to recognize them by the way they jump off the bat. I knew this one was out as soon as Jimmy hit it. Wohlers got beaten with his third-best pitch. Our whole dugout emptied to congratulate Jimmy. Believe me, I wanted to go out there too. But it's not proper protocol for a manager to be celebrating on the field, unless you're Tommy Lasorda and you can get away with hugging people. I'm not about to look for that kind of attention. And anyway, the game wasn't over. It was like I was numb at first. It took a moment for it to sink in that the score was now 6–6. It was still only the eighth inning.

I wound up using Aldrete as my pinch hitter. He grounded out. But I liked where this game was going. If you were the Braves, you had to believe you still had the hammer; you were still the home team in a tie game. But I figure they had to know the momentum had slipped away from them. It showed too. The Braves never again had a lead the rest of the Series. I think the sixth inning of the night before, when Cone had withstood the Atlanta rally, turned the Series around. It gave us momentum and confidence. But Jimmy's home run was nearly as big. It convinced us not only that we had played our way into a competitive World Series with the Braves, but also that we were going to win it.

Rivera shut down Atlanta for another inning by throwing his best pitch, the fastball, almost exclusively. Wohlers, meanwhile, should have been second-guessing himself. As Tim McCarver pointed out on the television broadcast after two men were out, "You haven't seen a slider yet from Mariano Rivera, have you?" Rivera was doing what he was supposed to be doing—he was throwing heat. It reminded me of the time I caught Steve Carlton and called for every pitch to be a fastball. When a pitcher is on with that kind of live fastball, it doesn't matter if the batter knows it's coming. He doesn't stand a chance.

Wohlers recovered in the ninth by getting out Jeter on a strike-out and Williams on a ground ball. We had two outs and nobody on base when Cecil cracked another hit—to right field yet again. Zim turned to me and asked, "What about pinch-running with Fox? We could steal second base easily off Wohlers's high leg kick." It wasn't a bad idea, but I really didn't like taking Cecil's bat out of a tie game. I also didn't like the idea of having to play Mariano Duncan at first base, an unfamiliar position for him, with the score tied. Before I had time to make a decision, Charlie Hayes smacked the next pitch into left field for a single.

Do I pinch-run for Cecil now? I really wrestled with that call. Cox went out to talk with Wohlers, and I still hadn't decided by the time he walked back to the dugout. Then Wohlers threw a pitch to Darryl. Finally I figured, hell, I've *got* to run for him. If Straw gets a hit and Cecil can't score from second base, I'll never forgive myself. So I sent Fox in to run for him. Straw did get a hit, though not the kind that could have scored Fox, it was another one of those blessed infield dribblers.

Now we had the bases loaded and two outs, and Duncan was facing Wohlers. Do I finally use Boggs here? Nope. Boggs was the only player I had left. If I used him and he didn't get the run in, then I might be in a situation in the tenth inning where I would have to let my pitcher hit. If this were the American League, I could have sent Boggs up there for Duncan. But I couldn't do that with the National League rules, not when my pitcher was batting and I'd need a pinch hitter. Duncan hit a rocket, but Dye, thanks to that overshifted alignment, caught the line drive in right field.

I planned to put Fox at second and Duncan at first base for the bottom of the ninth, but then Hayes came over to me and said, "Do you want me to play first base?"

"Have you ever done it?" I asked him.

"Yeah, this year with the Pirates," he said.

"Go ahead then," I said.

I liked that alignment better, with Duncan at second and Fox at third. Rivera went back out for another inning, even though he had thrown thirty-five pitches the night before. This was the World Series. I thought about all those times in April and May when people had asked me, "Did you think about using Rivera for another inning?" And I'd said, "If it was the World Series, I would." Well, here we were. It was something I never was faced with before. I had used that comment long enough, so now I had to put my money where my mouth was. I didn't like the idea of having him throw so many pitches, but there really was no decision, at least not until McGriff came up with two on and one out. That was when I brought in Graeme Lloyd, who some people, including our own media relations department, probably felt shouldn't even have been on our postseason roster. The media relations people didn't bother including a bio of Lloyd in our postseason media guide.

Lloyd had struggled big-time after we acquired him from Milwaukee in August. It turned out his elbow was killing him, but he didn't tell us. One day in Seattle he gave up a home run to Jeff Manto that cost us the ball game. Finally he admitted he was hurt. That really upset me. I told him, "Hell, you cost me a ball game." Pitching hurt or playing hurt is one thing. Playing stupid is something else. And Lloyd had been playing stupid.

In late September, as we were putting our post-season roster together, I called all my coaches into my office. I said, "All right, give me your ten-man staff." Everybody picked Dale Polley over Lloyd.

A few days later Zimmer said to me, "Give me your gut feeling. If you had to choose between Polley and Lloyd, who would you pick?"

"Lloyd," I said.

"So you have to do that," Zim said.

The next time we were voting on ten-man staffs, everybody picked Lloyd. I smiled. I knew Zim had been working the underground coaches' network. This is the way I saw it: Why had all of our scouts said Lloyd was the guy when we were looking for a left-hander? Once I found out he felt all right, I had to go back to the big picture and the scouting reports. And I talked to Phil Garner, who managed him in Milwaukee, and Bob Uecker, who worked as a broadcaster with the Brewers, and they gave me glowing reports on him as a person. So that was the gut call I made on the eve of the playoffs. He was healthy, and I wanted him.

I never dreamed he'd be *this* good, though. Lloyd had faced fifteen batters in October and retired fourteen of them, including McGriff on an inning-ending double play to get out of that ninth-inning jam. Welcome to extra innings. Cox decided not to push Wohlers into a third inning, so he brought in Steve Avery, the left-hander, to start the tenth inning. I assumed Cox had lost confidence in his other relievers, particularly Greg McMichael, who had given up a single, a home run, and a double to the three batters he faced in Game Three. So he gave the ball to Avery. Lloyd, who had never batted in the majors before, was due to hit second in the tenth inning. Zimmer asked me, "Who's going to hit?"

"Lloyd," I said.

"What about one of your other pitchers?" he asked.

Good point. If Leyritz, the leadoff batter, reached base, I was going to use Cone, who had experience batting in the National League, to bunt him to second. "Go put your spikes on," I told Cone, who dashed into the clubhouse to get ready. Then I thought if the score was still tied, I might use Jimmy Key to pitch two innings and save Wetteland, who was warming up, for later. I wanted to be prepared if this turned out to be a long extra-inning game. So I told Key to put his spikes on too.

Leyritz grounded out, so I left Lloyd in to hit, knowing that Cox still had Klesko, his big left-handed power threat, on his bench. But then I talked some more with Zim and Mel and decided to get Wetteland up again. "Hell, let's use him for two innings," I said. "Let's hope we score in his first inning and he'll save it in the second." Lloyd actually had a decent hack but grounded out.

Avery then ignited our rally with a huge blunder, considering he had two outs and nobody on: He walked Tim Raines, who had been 0-for-5 that night, on four pitches. I gave Raines the green light to steal—the sign that says take it when you want it. But Raines, to my disappointment, played it cautious and never made a break for the bag. The ice-cool kid, Jeter, fell behind 0-and-2 before working the count to two-and-two, then he rapped a single to left. I loved it. Now I had Bernie Williams hitting right-handed, which is by far his better side of the plate. Cox had two choices: bring in right-hander Brad Clontz to turn Williams around, or walk him. He knew I had Boggs to hit for Fox, who was due to hit after Bernie. I think Cox made the right call. He walked Bernie. Williams had been Mr. October for us, and one of the cardinal rules of managing is don't let the other team's best hitter beat you.

I stood there and said to Zim, "This is it. I've got Boggs." And he just said, "Yeah." Finally, that was the time to use my last player, a future Hall of Famer. I think being patient with my usage of players—making sure I didn't run myself out of players by holding on to Boggs like a trump card—helped win the game for us. "Boggsy!" I yelled, and he took off his jacket and got ready to hit. Now, I knew Boggs had struggled this year with runners on base and two out (.146). But you can throw those stats out the window in the postseason. I also knew he doesn't chase bad pitches. And I wondered what was going through his head. Ten years ago with the Boston Red Sox, the guy had been one strike away from being a world champion. Now here he was with a second chance.

As a manager, you almost never sit back and watch, unless it's the ninth inning and we have a lead. You always have to be thinking ahead. As Boggs walked to the plate, I was thinking about who the hell was going to pitch the bottom of the inning for us. Wetteland had been up and down like a yo-yo in the bullpen. In fact, after the game I felt so bad about that that I apologized to him for warming him up so many times. John just said to me, "I understand. You had no choice."

I figured if the game was still tied in the bottom of the tenth, I would use Lloyd. If we scored, it would be Wetteland. That whole time Zimmer was yacking away at me, firing questions left and right: "Where's the pitcher hitting? Who's pitching next inning? Who do they have left?" Sometimes I just had to say to him, "Shaddup." It was like a nutty Marx Brothers routine in the dugout.

Boggsy is a professional hitter. He didn't nibble at Avery's sliders off the plate, especially a dangerously close one—it was low—at two-and-two. With a full count and the bases loaded, Avery threw a fastball not nearly close enough in the strike zone to even tempt Boggs. Wade watched it for ball four and what had to be the biggest RBI of his great career. We had the lead for the first time all night, 7–6. Then Zim, Mel, and I all agreed: Wetteland would start the bottom of the inning. But then Cox made a move that put an end to our waffling about who should start the ninth inning. He pulled a double switch, putting Klesko at first base leading off and Clontz on the mound. Now it was obvious what to do: Lloyd for Klesko, with Wetteland after that.

Then Hayes hit a feeble little pop-up that, fittingly, Klesko dropped for an error, giving us another run. Beautiful. Now we were up 8–6, and Klesko would have to face Lloyd with nobody on base leading off the tenth. Naturally, Lloyd struck him out. As Zim said, "Klesko will be seeing that big lefty in his sleep." One thing we did perfectly in the Series was, we made Klesko a nonfactor. I knew he had done some damage against Cleveland in the 1995 World Series. But we completely took him out of this Series by starting a left-hander in five of the six games and by getting matchups against him late in the games with Lloyd, our suddenly invincible left-hander.

The rest of the game belonged to Wetteland. Big John added his usual flair for the exciting. The first batter, Andruw Jones, singled. I'm usually very cool in the dugout. I don't even pace. I've never showed a lot of emotion as a manager because I remember managers who cursed out loud or threw something if a guy struck out with the bases loaded or made an error. That always bothered me. Hell, I've been out there playing the game, and I know how hard it is. And the players on the bench are seeing their manager lose his cool, so they know when they're out there and mess up, he'll be doing the same thing. With two outs to go, though, I was nervous and jumpy in that dugout. I rearranged things in there, asking our trainer, Gene Monahan,

"Wasn't the Gatorade bucket over there yesterday when we won?" Of course, I'm not superstitious. Not at all. It was just in case somebody else was superstitious.

I was also a little nervous about Wetteland. He had struggled sometimes during the year after I would get him up and down a few times in the bullpen. Thankfully, he now closed the door, even if he did so somewhat gently rather than slamming it. He got two fly balls to the warning track in left field. On the second one Tim Raines looked for a moment as if he had misjudged the ball. He wound up falling backward on the track as he squeezed the last out. We won 8–6, the kind of score I had predicted before the game, with Rogers going to the mound. I had never seen my team with so much energy as it showed after that last out. I felt it too. That comeback was so stirring, I couldn't fall asleep that night until four-thirty in the morning.

In the clubhouse I hugged everybody in sight and yelled things like "How about Graeme Lloyd! How about David Weathers! How about Jeff Nelson! You guys are great! This is a great team!" I made sure I hugged Kenny Rogers too. I thought about that great Game Six of the 1975 World Series, when Carlton Fisk wrapped a home run around the fair side of the foul pole, and I told Zim, who had been coaching third base for the Red Sox then, "This is going to go down as one of the greatest ever, just like that Carlton Fisk game! Except we're going to win this damned thing!"

I was just so excited. I wasn't even thinking about tomorrow. The Series was tied two games to two, but I felt so good about it because we were guaranteed to go back to New York, which was huge for us, even though we had lost the first two games there. After we lost the first game, I had said all we had to do was win two out of the next four to get it back home. I knew there would be less pressure on us for Games Six and Seven than there had been for games Games One and Two.

The feeling I had after Game Four was unbelievable. I felt bulletproof. There are things you do right and things you do wrong—like when I was trying to decide about pinch-running for Fielder. I'd made up my mind after that first pitch to Straw. But if that first pitch had been a base hit and Cecil hadn't scored, I would have looked like a dummy. Now nobody noticed it. When you're hot, you get away with things like that. That's what made me think I was bulletproof.

After the celebration in the clubhouse, I just sat there at my desk in the manager's office with a smile on my face and talked with some friends on the phone. Everything seemed to be happening for a reason. Leyritz hit that three-run home run, and it didn't even surprise me. Hayes hit that dribbler that took a right-hand turn fair, and strange as it was, it seemed that was the way it was meant to be. It was weird. I had had this little thought in my head throughout the playoffs and the World Series that would not go away. It was never so strong as in those euphoric moments after Game Four. Over and over again it went like this: I always see good things happen for other people. Why can't they happen to me now? I've waited so long for this. At this point everything is equal. Why *not* me?

CHAPTER 10

On Top of the World

I WAS SO EXHAUSTED, WHEN I WOKE up after Game Four, that I didn't want to leave my hotel for lunch. Then my friend Ed Maull called me up and reminded me that we had gone out to lunch before both Game Three and Game Four—and both games had turned out to be victories. "We *have* to have lunch," he said. I agreed. I wasn't going to screw it up now. My wife went shopping, with her sisters Mary, Katie, and Rosie, and I went to lunch at the Buckhead Diner with Ed and two other friends, Arthur Sando and Dr. Joe Platania. As we drove to the diner I sensed that Dr. Joe wanted to provide his usual help to me regarding my lineup.

"So, what are you going to do tonight?" he asked me.

"I don't know," I lied. I didn't want to tell anybody.

"I've got your lineup for you," Dr. Joe said, and he proceeded to run through his batting order. We were facing a tough right-handed pitcher, John Smoltz, that night, so he had most of my left-handed hitters, including Boggs, back in his lineup. "Now, who are you going to play?" he asked me.

"I'm not going to tell you," I said.

Deep down, I knew I had some very tough decisions to make that were guaranteed to make somebody very unhappy. When I got to the ballpark around three o'clock, I asked Zimmer, "Who would you play?" He said, "O'Neill, Boggs, Martinez . . ." I looked at him and shook my head. "Nope. Can't do that," I said. I told him I had decided I was going to leave Hayes, Fielder, and Raines in my lineup. He gave me that bug-eyed look of his. I knew he was very surprised. Against Smoltz, the 1996 Cy Young award winner, who was twenty-eight and eight, including his four postseason wins—I was keeping three of my best left-handed hitters on the bench: two batting champions (Boggs and O'Neill) and our top RBI guy over the course of the season (Martinez).

I've never been the type of manager who just posts the lineup in the clubhouse without explanation, not when I have these kinds of decisions to make. So one by one I called the players who weren't starting into my office. First I talked to Boggs. I explained that I liked the way Hayes was swinging the bat, and that Hayes had had decent success against Smoltz when he played in the National League. I could tell Boggsy was disappointed, but he took it pretty well. Then I talked to Tino. I told him Cecil looked like he was so locked in and was swinging such a hot bat that I had to play him. Tino was clearly angry. He listened to what I had to say and walked out, hardly saying a word.

And then I brought in O'Neill. That was the toughest call for me. I was upset with Raines. In Game Three we had been leading 2–0 in the fifth inning when Raines, with one out, got doubled off first base on a fly ball that was caught in right-center field. He was past second base when the ball was caught, so he stopped, looked at the outfielder who caught the ball, and figured "I can't get back." Then he realized he *could* have made make it back, but it was too late. He had made a mistake, and he knew it. Since then he had gone 0-for-7. I decided I wanted Raines batting leadoff anyway, as he had in our wins in Games Three and Four. When I broke the news to O'Neill, he was devastated—just crushed. Paulie had been busting his ass for us for weeks with a bad leg, and here I had just slapped him in the face. His reaction was totally different from Tino's. Tino was mad. Paulie was just re-signed. He looked very down. He walked out of my office with his head bowed and his shoulders slouched.

Only a few minutes later Zimmer walked into my office. "Paulie's down," he said.

"Yeah, I know," I said. Then I started to kick an idea around in my head. I said to Zim, "Let's play him. Let's play O'Neill."

"Instead of Strawberry?" Zim asked.

"No. Instead of Raines," I said.

"Yeah, you can do that," he said.

"Tell Paulie I want to see him," I said.

Zim went for O'Neill. When O'Neill came back into my office, I said to him, "Manager's prerogative. I changed my mind. You're playing."

I had changed my mind because of what I read out of Paul's body language. What it told me was that by not playing him, I might have lost him completely. His confidence and his energy might have been so shot at that point that he might not have done me much good for the rest of the Series. But Paulie had been too important to our club all year for that to happen.

A manager has to be very flexible reading players and reacting to situations. I may have been a better manager in 1996 than before only because some things worked out, but I always felt that I've managed with the intent to win the game at hand as opposed to managing to answer questions afterward. As George Kissell taught me, you can't go by "the book" just to cover your ass. The manager is the one who's with the players every day and gets a sense of what they're all about. And there are days when they're not the same as they were the day before, and you have to have a feel for that. I will say that I probably spent more time hanging around the players in the clubhouse and the trainers' room in 1996 than I had in the past. It brought me closer to the players and that meant a lot to me, especially after my relationship with the St. Louis players had soured in 1995.

Game Five, like Game Four, turned out to be another one of those classic chess matches where I had to rely on my experience and instincts, not just the comfort of percentages. Smoltz started off in typically dominant fashion by striking out six of our first nine batters. But then in the fourth inning, two of my surprise starters, Hayes and Fielder, combined to get us a 1–0 lead. Hayes hit a fly ball into right-center field, where Marquis Grissom and Jermaine Dye converged. Neither one really took charge of the play, and the ball wound up bouncing off Grissom's glove for a two-base error. Then Bernie Williams, playing perfect situational baseball, moved Charlie to third with a grounder to the right side. Then Cecil smoked a double off the left-field wall to put us ahead.

Andy Pettitte was even better than Smoltz. He had a four-hit shutout through eight innings. Everybody expected me to give Wetteland the ball in the ninth inning to close out a 1–0 game. But Pettitte hadn't even thrown a hundred pitches, and Chipper Jones and Fred McGriff, both of whom hit right-handers better, were Atlanta's first two batters of the ninth inning. I wanted Pettitte to face them. There was one potential problem, though: We were playing under National League rules and Pettitte was due to bat fifth in the top of the ninth. Should I take him out for a pinch hitter if his spot came up?

After two outs Mariano Duncan was on first base with Jimmy Leyritz batting against Mark Wohlers, with Pettitte on deck. I gave Duncan the steal sign, figuring if he was thrown out it was no big deal, and I wouldn't have to decide whether to pinch hit for Pettitte. It was worth the gamble. I guess I was on such a roll that everything was going our way. Duncan was safe. Naturally the Braves decided to walk Leyritz. Wohlers, however, threw ball four all the way to the backstop, advancing Duncan yet another base. Now we had runners on first and third, two outs, and my pitcher was up. I made up my mind to let Pettitte hit, even though I had Boggs and Raines on my bench. I explained to Zimmer why I wanted Andy to stay in the game. "Am I crazy or what?" I asked Zim, who said, "No, it makes sense."

One obnoxious fan next to the dugout apparently didn't agree. He was screaming, "Hey, Torre! What about Boggs? What about Boggs, you dummy!" Zim, as only Zim can do, turned around and snapped, "Sit down you asshole!"

Meanwhile, back in New York, Frank was probably questioning me, too, as he watched the game from his hospital bed. A friend of mine from New York, Jack Kennedy, was sitting with Frank during the three games in Atlanta. Frank would scream at the television whenever I made a move he didn't like. "You idiot," he'd say. "You moron. Why did you do that?" Poor Jack. He kept one eye on the game and one eye on Frank's heart monitor, worried sick about both of them.

Ali was at the game, sitting next to Pettitte's wife, Laura. When Laura saw Andy walking to the plate to hit, she said, "Oh, no. Oh, no. Andy never pitches the ninth inning. He always takes him out. What is he doing?" Laura had seen enough excitement for eight innings and wanted to relax for the last three outs. My wife didn't have an answer for her. Like a lot of people, she didn't know what I was doing either. But she told Laura, "Don't worry. Andy will be fine."

More important, Andy had thought he was coming out of the game too. I didn't find that out until later. I figured I had given him the message when I left him in the on-deck circle with Leyritz batting. The message was, This is your game. I guess Andy didn't get it. If I had known at the time that he expected to be taken out of the game, I would have talked to him, because once you think you're out— like Koosman did back with the Mets—you let your guard down. Andy actually had a couple of decent hacks up at the plate, but he eventually flied out for the third out.

In the bottom of the ninth Pettitte really put me on the hot seat when he hung a pitch to Jones, who knocked it into left field for a double. The tying run was on second base with no outs. I let Pettitte face McGriff, and he got him out on a grounder, though Jones moved to third. Then I called for Wetteland. Big John got an out and kept Jones at third with one pitch, getting Javy Lopez on a grounder to Hayes. Now we needed one more out to win the game. Bobby Cox had two pinch hitters ready: first Klesko, and then I figured it would be Terry Pendleton. I decided it was time to walk out to talk to Wetteland. I remembered a game we had lost to Boston in July and I didn't want to repeat the same mistake that cost us that game.

Wetteland had pitched the ninth inning in Boston with an 11–9 lead. He walked Tim Naehring with one out, so I sent Mel Stottlemyre to the mound to remind him to be aggressive. That was the big mistake. Mike Stanley hit a double, but then Wetteland struck out Kevin Mitchell. Two outs. Now what do I do? Pitch to Reggie Jefferson, who was batting .375, or Troy O'Leary? I couldn't talk to Wetteland about it, because if you visit a pitcher twice in the same inning, you have to take him out. I held up four fingers, telling Wetteland to intentionally walk Jefferson. I could see John slump; his body language told me he didn't like the idea. With the bases loaded John grooved a fastball to O'Leary on the first pitch. He later said he was trying to get ahead of O'Leary with no room on base to put him. But that's where he was wrong. Even if he walked O'Leary, he still would have had a one-run lead. I would have told him that, if only we had not already used up that first visit to the mound. O'Leary ripped a double, tying the game. Jeff Frye then hit a single to give Boston a 12–11 win. I felt absolutely awful that night. I decided then that whenever Wetteland was in position to walk someone intentionally, I would talk to him.

When I got to the mound, I said to John, "I'm here to ask you a question. Would you feel better pitching to Klesko or Pendleton?"

"Um . . ." John hesitated. That was enough for me.

"Put him on," I said. "Go get Pendleton."

So John walked Klesko. I didn't worry about putting the winning run on base, not when it's a guy like Klesko, who can hit a home run at any time. Cox surprised me a little by sending up Luis Polonia to bat instead of Pendleton. Polonia fouled off about six fastballs in a row. Zimmer turned to me and said, "Wouldn't it be nice if John threw one of those curveballs right now?" I said, "Yeah, but I don't want one in the dirt that goes back to the screen either." I think John was worried about that, too, because a passed ball would have easily scored Jones and would have tied the game. He kept pumping fastballs until Polonia finally put one in play, a flyball to right-center field.

"That's an out," I thought to myself. But then I saw O'Neill keep running back for it. And then it looked like he stumbled—I thought he stepped in a hole or something. And then, with every ounce of strength that was left in those gimpy legs, O'Neill made one last stride at the edge of the warning track. He extended his arm and opened his glove. If he catches the ball, I thought, we win 1–0 and take a three-games-to-two lead in the Series. If he doesn't, we lose 2–1, the Braves take a three-games-to-two lead, and I will be skewered for letting Pettitte bat in the ninth inning. O'Neill, who wasn't supposed to be in the lineup, whose body language had caused me to change my mind about playing him, caught the ball. We were an amazing 8–0 on the road in the postseason, needing only one more win at Yankee Stadium to be world champions.

I felt great flying back on our charter flight that night—taking with me those unsightly peppers, still in the same unopened bag, of course. It's funny how when you win and hardly get any sleep, you still feel terrific. When you lose, you can sleep all night and still feel lousy when you wake up. By the time I got to the door of my house, it was five-fifteen in the morning. Thirty minutes later the telephone rang. It was Columbia-Presbyterian. They had a heart for Frank. A twenty-eight-year-old man from the Bronx had died from a brain disease and had donated his major organs. It looked like a good match. They were taking Frank down to surgery at six-thirty. I was terrified at first, thinking about the operation. But then I thought, Hell, this is what we'd been waiting for. There was nothing I could do but wait. Dr. Eric Rose called me twice to tell me how the operation was going. I'd doze off a little in between calls. And then, at eleven-thirty, he called to tell me it was over. It looked good. Dr. Mehmet Oz, who had placed the heart in Frank's chest cavity, said the heart took to Frank like a fish to water. I couldn't believe what was happening. We were one victory away from the World Series, and Frank had received a heart from a man named Oz. I didn't know whether to laugh, cry, or click my heels three times. Dr. Rose told me Frank was in recovery, still not alert because of all the drugs in him. I left for the ballpark for our voluntary workout, after about ninety minutes of sleep.

I went to see Frank at about seven o'clock that night. Reggie Jackson and his agent, Matt Merola, were there too. Frank had tubes in him all over the place. He couldn't talk, but he nodded to my questions and wrote me notes. "Nice going," he wrote. And "No visitors." I was there about twenty minutes when I decided to let him rest. I bent over and kissed him on the cheek. Soon after we left, Frank's wife slipped his 1957 World Series ring back on his finger. Everything seemed right in the world.

I drove home and picked up Ali, who had taken a commercial flight back to New York, and we went out to dinner. When we came home, Ali checked the messages on our machine.

"Joe, you've got to listen to this," she said. "Someone is saying he's your brother, but it doesn't sound like him."

I played the tape. She was right—it didn't sound like Frank saying, "This is your brother. I just wanted to talk to you." It was a sick trick if some-one else was pretending to be Frank. So I called the hospital and asked, "Did Frank try to call me?" They told me yes, he did. They arranged for Frank to call me back. And when he did, this is what he told me: "I need six tickets to tomorrow's game for my new friends here. I'll send somebody over there tomorrow to pick them up." Great! I thought. The old wheeler-dealer is back. I knew he was starting to feel better already.

I didn't sleep much that night either. I was so thrilled about Frank and the World Series that after about two hours of sleep, I woke up full of energy. I was running on fumes just about the entire post-season. I look at pictures of myself taken during the World Series, and I can see I'm totally exhausted—I just didn't know it at the time. I arrived at Yankee Stadium at eleven-thirty in the morning on Satur-day, more than eight hours before Game Six. The first thing I did when I sat down at my desk was to call my wife and ask her if we had enough cham-pagne in our house for a party. Ali said no, we would need more. So I called a wine shop in Bronx-ville run by Alfredo Cruz, whom Rusty Staub had introduced me to during the season. I ordered two cases of champagne to be delivered to my house. Confident? The way I looked at it, nothing would be open until Monday if I waited until after the game to order champagne. But I have to admit that I felt like I was on a roll. If you can't feel confident after winning three games in Atlanta and with your brother finally getting a heart transplant, when can you?

And then it really hit me, sitting in my office before Game Six: My team could win the World Series tonight. Suddenly, I became as nervous as I've ever been in my entire life. Reggie Jackson had been checking on me throughout the postseason. Every once in a while he'd say to me, "Joe, you look so calm. How do you feel?" And I'd say, "I'm fine. I'm all right." But when I saw Reggie before Game Six, I didn't even wait for him to ask.

"Reggie," I said, "I'm not calm anymore."

He smiled. Reggie liked that. He had played in enough big games to know that a little nervousness is a natural reaction.

Zimmer must have been confident. He came in my office and said, "You know, when we won our division title with the Cubs, we took a victory lap around the field. I thought that worked out great. You might want to think about it."

The best feeling I had coming into the game was knowing that our pitching was virtually at full strength. Everybody in the bullpen had had two days off except for Wetteland, and I knew he was fine. He had had one day off after pitching in the ninth inning of Game Five. The only one I was uncertain about was Jeff Nelson. We could not use him in Game Five because his elbow bothered him, and we weren't sure if he was available for Game Six. I was relieved that I had a fresh Mariano Rivera. And I knew that even if we didn't win, we could come back the next day with the same relievers available.

The matchup of starting pitchers was a repeat of Game Two: Jimmy Key against Greg Maddux. As Jimmy walked out to the mound for the first inning, I had one thought on my mind: Get me through the sixth inning. If we kept the game close through the sixth, and especially if we managed a lead, I loved the idea of turning the game over to Mo and John.

Maddux was sharp again. When he cruised through the first two innings in perfect order, he had faced thirty-five batters in this World Series while allowing the ball out of the infield only eight times. But then, leading off the third inning of a scoreless game, O'Neill came through. He ripped a hard double into the right-field corner. That made me feel even better about changing my mind about playing Paul in Game Five; now he was there when we needed him. With no outs, Duncan did a perfect job of moving the runner to third when he grounded out to second base. With Girardi batting, Maddux proved that even the greatest pitchers make mistakes. He left a pitch up in the strike zone, and Girardi belted it to the wall in center field for a triple and a 1–0 lead.

I was so happy for Joe. I hadn't had much to do with constructing the Yankees after I was hired—George and Bob had done most of that work while asking my opinion on some players. But being a former catcher, the one thing I pushed for was getting a good defensive catcher who knew how to handle pitchers. Mike Stanley had been the Yankees catcher before I got there. I knew he was a good hitter, but he looked inconsistent behind the plate, from what I saw on television and some videos the Yankees gave me. I've always liked my catcher to give me defense first, offense second. I talked with Zimmer, who had managed Girardi with the Cubs, and Mel Stottlemyre. We agreed Girardi was the best defensive catcher in the National League. I liked his approach to hitting—he sprayed the ball to all fields—and he could run a little bit. As I had been, Girardi was a player rep during the strike. I think that's one of the reasons the Colorado Rockies made him available to us in a trade. The New York fans had hated the deal because Stanley, whom we allowed to leave as a free agent, had been a popular player. Joe was heckled when he came to our fan festival in January. But he won over everyone with his consistency, his hustle—and especially his big triple off Maddux.

We kept the rally going. Cox thought I would squeeze on the first pitch to Jeter—he called a pitch-out—but Derek was swinging too hot a bat for me to give up an out. Jeter knocked the next pitch into center field for a single, to drive in Girardi. Then Jeter stole second base and, after Boggsy flied out, scored on a single by Bernie. We had a 3–0 lead on Maddux.

Jimmy was pitching a gutsy game. He decided he wasn't going to come close to making the kind of mistake Maddux made to Girardi. If he was going to miss with his pitches, it was going to be outside the strike zone, where he wouldn't get hurt. He threw the majority of his pitches with that mindset, which usually bothers me, but he stayed out of a big inning. He really nibbled in the fourth inning, when he forced in a run for Atlanta with a bases-loaded walk. With our lead down to 3–1 and the bases full with one out, Jimmy got Terry Pendleton to ground into a double play. That was enormous. Jimmy was one pitch away from coming out of the game; if he had thrown ball four or allowed a hit, I would have gone to my bullpen.

The biggest inning for me, as usual, was the sixth. There was magic in the number six for me, a guy who switched from uniform number 9 in St. Louis to number 6 in New York, trying to win the world championship in '96 in six games. See what I mean about destiny? In Game Three Cone had pitched out of that jam in the sixth inning; in Game Four we had started our comeback from a 6–0 deficit in the sixth inning; in Game Five Pettitte had preserved the 1–0 lead with two exceptional fielding plays in the sixth inning; and in Game Six I would need three pitchers to get me through the sixth inning.

Key gave up a leadoff double to Chipper Jones. I immediately started David Weathers and Graeme Lloyd throwing in the bullpen. Jimmy got McGriff out on a ground ball on a play in which Chipper advanced to third. With Nelson still a little tender,

I called on Weathers to get Javy Lopez. Weathers was magnificent. He struck out Lopez on three pitches for the second out. He made good pitches to Andruw Jones next, but the rookie was patient and drew a walk. When the Braves sent Ryan Klesko to bat, I called on Lloyd one more time. This matchup was a little too exciting. Lloyd threw ball one. And then ball two. And then he left a slider on the inside part of the plate. It was a mistake pitch. Klesko is strong enough to have knocked out a bulb atop the right-field light tower with a pitch like that. He had the pitch to hit but just missed it. He popped it up. We had dodged a bullet. I let out a big sigh of relief. We had made it through the sixth inning with a 3–1 lead. My work was almost over. It was as easy as sticking to the Formula after that.

I did make one more move. I took Boggs out of the game in the seventh inning and put Charlie Hayes at third base. I had started Boggs over Hayes just on a hunch. It was a move based totally on a feeling I had, not on statistics. After Boggs batted three times without a hit, I needed my best defensive team on the field to protect the lead. While Boggsy has very good hands, he doesn't have the same range that Charlie does. I knew Wade had been with us all year and wanted to be on the field for the last out, but he should know as well as anybody that there is no room for sentiment at a time like that. He played on the 1986 Red Sox team that was one strike away from winning the world championship against the Mets. Boston manager John McNamara left Bill Buckner and his wobbly legs at first base, even though during the regular season he had regularly replaced Buckner with Dave Stapleton, a better fielder, to protect late-inning leads. This time McNamara wanted Buckner to be on the field for a world championship celebration. I was surprised to see Buckner out there, especially because Johnny Mac had made the defensive change all year. Of course, the Mets won the game when Buckner let a ground ball through his legs.

Rivera, after walking his first batter on four pitches, blew away six straight hitters to get us to the ninth inning. I turned to Stottlemyre and said, "What about Rivera in the ninth?" Mel looked at me as if he were about to have a heart attack. I smiled at him, letting him in on my little joke. "We haven't done it all year, have we?" I said.

The ninth inning belonged to Big John. He struck out Andruw Jones. One out. Klesko hit a ground ball to Jeter's left. Jeter has a problem with balls to his left because he tries to catch everything with two hands, rather than stabbing the ball with his glove hand. Two hands are preferred for balls hit right at you, but you can't reach as far to balls at your side if you reach with both hands rather than one. Derek, with his abbreviated reach, saw Klesko's grounder kick off the end of his glove for a base hit. Then Pendleton stroked a single to right field, sending Klesko to third. The tying runs were on base. The next batter was Polonia, who had battled his ass off against Wetteland before making that last out of Game Five. This time John overpowered him, striking him out quickly. Two outs. One out to go for the world championship. I was sitting on my hands in the dugout, nervous as hell on the inside. I grew more nervous when Marquis Grissom grounded a single into right field. Klesko scored to cut our lead to 3–2. Well, I thought, we've been doing it all year like this. Another one-run game. Why should this one be any different?

Mark Lemke batted next. The tying run was on second base and the go-ahead run at first. Lemke is one of those tough hitters you hate to see up there in these situations. He's a clutch postseason player who puts the ball in play. Lemke lifted a pop-up next to the Atlanta dugout on the third-base side. Hayes reached over the railing of a photographers' well and barely missed catching the foul ball. I turned to Zimmer and asked, "What do you think? Should I go out there or send Mel out there just to give John a breather? Settle him down?"

"Naw," Zimmer said. "He's going to get him out on this next pitch."

Then John threw a great pitch: a hard fastball away. Lemke lofted another pop-up near the Braves dugout. As soon as that ball went up, I knew this one was in play. I've watched too many games from the same seat at Yankee Stadium not to know when a ball is going in the stands and when it's not. I held my breath. I had waited thirty-seven years since I'd signed my first big league contract for this

295

very moment. And now it seemed like it took another thirty-seven years for the baseball to come down. Finally it landed in Hayes's glove. And then I couldn't see anything. Zimmer, Stottlemyre, and the rest of my coaches jumped on me and started beating on me. I started screaming—just screaming with joy.

As soon as I got out from under the pile in the dugout, I ran on the field. This celebration was one I definitely was going to take part in. After all those years of painfully watching other people have their fun, now it was my turn. Months after it happened, I still get choked up when I see videos of our celebration after the last out. It was always Michael Jordan and the Bulls, or the Dallas Cowboys, or so many other teams piling on each other. Now whenever I see video of my Yankees team doing it, I think, Wow, that's us. That's really us. It gives me goose bumps.

After a minute or two of hugging my players, I remembered Zimmer's suggestion about a victory lap. I told Leyritz, "Let's take it around the field!" We headed toward the right-field seats, but when we turned around, no one was following us. So Jimmy and I went back to the crowd of players and said, "Let's go," and they all took off for left field. I was a little frightened as we ran near the mounted police, who were on the field for crowd control. The previous year, after I had been fired by St. Louis, I visited the paddock area of Saratoga and learned you should never walk behind a horse—if it gets scared it can kill you with one swift kick. I made sure to keep a safe distance from those horses.

We ran around the edge of the warning track, waving to the fans. I'll never forget seeing such happiness on their faces. As much as they loved the victory lap, I think we enjoyed it even more. We ran all the way around the outfield and along the first-base seats. I stopped when I got next to our dugout and my box, where my daughters Tina and Lauren and my son Michael were sitting. Tina was crying like a baby. I hugged all of them. My wife and Andrea were sitting farther back; I always made sure my baby was protected from foul balls by the screen behind home plate.

Zimmer came up to me after he finished the lap. He was breathing heavily. "Joe," he said, "remember when I told you about that lap we took with the Cubs? We walked. You damn near killed me out there."

The next two or three hours in the clubhouse were a blur of interviews, hugs, kisses, champagne showers, and cigar smoke. I was so busy running around that I missed the congratulatory call from President Clinton, though he did track me down the next day in my office. I do remember standing on a wooden platform in the back of the clubhouse holding the World Series trophy with George, when I heard someone hollering louder than any one else, "Wooooo!" I recognized my wife's voice. I turned, and when our eyes met as she ran to me she yelled, "Yes! Yes!" I started crying all over again with her in my arms.

It was close to two o'clock in the morning before I decided to leave. Ali had long since headed home with Andrea and made sure our nephew Jeff had taken my car keys. I was going to take a shower, but then I thought, Why bother? I walked out of Yankee Stadium in my champagne-soaked uniform. I had taken about five or six steps when the crowd that was still milling around outside started cheering. I jumped into the back of a car waiting for me, a beat-up BMW belonging to Dr. Joe. Arthur Sando was sitting in the front. Fans quickly surrounded the car. They pounded on it in excitement, and for a moment I feared they were going to turn it over. With some police help we were able to make it out of there and back to my house. I walked in the door to see my home packed with people. And I had no idea who half of them were.

I didn't talk with Frank until the morning after our game, Sunday. He was in intensive care, so I couldn't call him. I had to wait for his call. When he did call, it was one of the rare times when I heard his voice crack with emotion. For years Frank used to have fun needling me about never having been to the World Series. Anytime I thought I was smarter or better than him, he'd remind me, "I've been to the World Series twice and got my ring; you don't have any." What could I say? He was right. This telephone call was the first time I could talk to my brother like I was on the same level as him. This time he had nothing to complain about with me.

In a soft weakened voice, Frank said, "Nice going, kid." Those three simple words meant more to me than all the thousands of flattering stories, headlines, and pictures ever devoted to me.

The next day, Monday, I was invited to appear on *The Late Show with David Letterman.* I wore the same suit I had worn to the press conference when I was introduced as manager of the Yankees—only five days shy of exactly one year that I had gone from Clueless Joe to national celebrity. I brought Cardenal's lucky peppers with me, which by then were grotesquely shriveled, and Letterman's people placed them between David's and my chair before the taping in anticipation of making them a topic of discussion. I never did get around to talking about them. Toward the end of my interview I was ambushed with champagne spray by Leyritz, Boggs, and O'Neill. I had no idea they would do that. I just threw my hands up as if to say, "Go to it, guys." After the show I figured I would go home to change clothes before I met Ali, Joe Molloy, and Bob Watson and his wife for dinner. But Letterman's people had a complete new outfit waiting for me, including socks, underwear, shirt, tie, and a blue double-breasted suit. Amazingly, other than the pants being an inch too long, the clothes fit perfectly. A few days later they delivered my freshly cleaned suit to my home—but not the peppers.

They still may be rotting next to David's desk, for all I know.

On the morning after the Letterman show, I had the honor of ringing the bell to open trading on the New York Stock Exchange. I signed so many autographs and posed for so many pictures that it took an hour just to walk across the floor of the exchange. It was a thrill to be there, and it made me wonder: If Frank hadn't encouraged me to be a catcher in those days when I was working for the American Exchange, I would be working on the floor instead of being congratulated on being a world champion.

I had to hustle out of the exchange because I had an important date: a ticker-tape parade for the team down lower Broadway in Manhattan. While we waited in a tent for the parade to start, I was thrilled to meet one of my favorite recording artists, Placido Domingo. I was happy to see my mother-in-law and father-in-law there too. I'm sorry my parents were not alive to share in my happiness, but Ali's parents have become such special people in my life that it was wonderful for me to see them at the parade.

I rode on a float with Bob Watson and my coaches. I was stunned at the sheer number of people who had turned out along the parade route. The police estimated that three million people were there. I saw nothing but smiling faces as far as I could see. When we reached each intersection, I would look down the cross street and see people lined up for what must have been a quarter of a mile just to get a glimpse of us as we rode by. As a native New Yorker, I recall the ticker-tape parades given to General Douglas MacArthur and to the Apollo 11 astronauts, though I must say, as a St. Louis Cardinals player at the time, I didn't pay much attention to the one for the 1969 world champion Mets. I was awed by those parades as they made their way through what is known as the Canyon of Heroes. No city in the world but New York can put on such a spectacle. To be a part of one myself—one of the biggest such parades ever— made me proud to be a New Yorker and proud to be a Yankee. Add me to the list of people who believe there's no better place to win than in New York, especially when it's your hometown. I had to ask myself, Is it really you? Are you really a part of this? It was like an out-of-body experience.

For days, even weeks, I floated in a thick, dreamy haze of utter happiness. I wore a silly grin on my face every waking moment—probably in my sleep too. I was the honorary starter with Mayor Rudy Giuliani of the New York Marathon, then took a helicopter ride over the Verrazano Bridge in the brilliant light of a crisp morning as the mass of runners spilled like water from one side of the bridge to the other. I attended a Knicks game at Madison Square Garden with Ali, David Cone, and his wife. We received an overwhelming standing ovation when we were introduced to the crowd. We were touched by the way people responded to us.

Whenever I went out in public, even shopping with Ali, I felt people's eyes following me all the time.

The high still hasn't worn off. I feel a thoroughly satisfying sense of accomplishment and exoneration. The most amazing part is that it is so lasting. Not a day goes by where I don't feel it, whether I'm reminded by others or feel it myself. It's with me from my first cup of coffee in the morning to my last sip of wine at night. It's so powerful that I'm glad such happiness came to me later in life. I can understand how people get carried away with success. At fifty-six, I'm too old to change.

I have never been happier in my life, and yet when I say those words I feel guilty. It's difficult to admit feeling so enchanted when I know that Rocco died in the middle of my championship season. I thought about him often during our drive to the World Series. In the ninth innings of tense games, when all I could do was watch, I would think about Rocco and the way he showed me what a loving husband and father could be. I thought about how, as children, my friend Matt Borzello and I would bring him sandwiches and plates of food from home when he was on police duty; he always was happy to see me, but never more than I was to see him. Whenever I thought about Rocco in those moments of anxiety in the dugout, I became calm and relaxed. I wish he could have been there to feel the excitement of every victory and to taste the sweetness of the champagne. But the way I see it, maybe he had to be up there in heaven for all of this to happen. Maybe in his own way Rocco made possible all the wonderful things that we clumsily ascribe to destiny.

Ali preferred that I quit this managing grind after the World Series, though she knew I would honor my contract. I understood what she was thinking. I had reached my lifelong dream and we had a beautiful girl nearing her first birthday to take care of. But there are more people to think about than just me. We won as a team. I didn't want to walk away from the players, the staff, and the special feeling we created in New York. I want to defend our championship. It will be invigorating to go back out there on the field as a world champion. It's like buying a beautiful new suit. Now you want to wear it.

One day in December, with the glow of the coming Christmas everywhere, George called me to a meeting in his office at Yankee Stadium. It was the meeting for which I had been waiting my whole life. I sat down in a chair at his conference table, the same chair in which I had been sitting when George told me we didn't dare go into a doubleheader in Cleveland with two rookie starting pitchers. Bob Watson and Arthur Richman were sitting with us. On the table before us, sparkling like long-lost treasures, nearly a dozen styles of World Series championship rings shimmered against the smooth polish of the wood table. Some of them were inscribed "Watson," some of them were inscribed "Steinbrenner," and most of them were inscribed

"Torre." It was real now. It was time to choose what style of ring we wanted.

"After we decide on this one," I told George, "then we're going to decide on Tuesday's ring, right? One for every day of the week?"

George laughed. Then I turned serious for a minute. George understood about my promise, twenty-four years ago to Frank, that I would replace his 1958 World Series ring with one of my own someday. I didn't want to leave anything to chance though. I wanted to be on record as requesting a ring for Frank.

"Don't forget," I told George, "I want to buy an extra ring for Frank. I've got to have one for Frank."

"Don't worry," George said. "We'll make sure of that."

I had told Frank, a short time after we won the World Series, that I intended to make good on my promise. I told him I was going to order a second ring inscribed "Torre" and give it to him. I knew he planned to give it to his son, Frankie. Frank pretended it was no big deal.

"Aw, you don't have to worry about getting me a regular ring," he said. "Just get me a cheaper one."

"Don't you worry about it," I said. "I'll handle it."

It was fun playing with the different styles of rings. Bob, George, Arthur, and I slipped them on and off our fingers, holding our hands out to admire the beauty of each one. We all kept coming back to the same ring. The interlocking "NY" of the Yankees was highlighted in diamonds on the top. One side featured a raised replica of the world championship trophy and the number 23, representing the number of world championships won by the franchise. The other side was inscribed with three words that characterized the spirit of our ball club: "Courage. Tradition. Pride." George especially liked that touch. This was going to be the ring.

I liked it, too, but I had one small change in mind, a change everyone else immediately agreed on. I thought about the way my Yankees never gave up, the way no deficit, no matter how big or how late, was too big for us to conquer. And I thought about the connection my team shared with my two brothers: Rocco, how he died, and Frank, how he lives. The words will be forever etched in gold.

"Courage. Tradition. Heart."

ABOUT THE AUTHORS

JOE TORRE was born and raised in Brooklyn, New York. A nine-time all-star for the Milwaukee and Atlanta Braves, the St. Louis Cardinals, and the New York Mets, he retired in 1977 to become a manager. On November 1, 1995, he was named manager of the New York Yankees. He lives in New York with his wife, Alice, and their daughter, Andrea Rae.

TOM VERDUCCI is a senior writer for *Sports Illustrated*. He lives with his wife, Kirsten, and two sons, Adam and Benjamin, in New Jersey.